THE MATILDA EFFECT

ELLIE IRVING

CORGI BOOKS

CORGI BOOKS

UK | USA | Canada | Ireland | Australia
India | New Zealand | South Africa

Corgi Books is part of the Penguin Random House group of companies
whose addresses can be found at global.penguinrandomhouse.com.

www.penguin.co.uk
www.puffin.co.uk
www.ladybird.co.uk

Penguin
Random House
UK

First published 2017
005

Set in 13/19.5 pt Bembo Book MT Std by Jouve (UK), Milton Keynes
Printed in Great Britain by Clays Ltd, Elcograf S.p.A.
A CIP catalogue record for this book is available from the British Library

ISBN: 978–0–552–56837–1

All correspondence to:
Corgi Books
Penguin Random House Children's
80 Strand, London WC2R 0RL

MIX
Paper from
responsible sources
FSC® C018179
www.fsc.org

Penguin Random House is committed to a
sustainable future for our business, our readers
and our planet. This book is made from Forest
Stewardship Council® certified paper.

For Mum

Because Barbara tries very hard

CONTENTS

THE 'WHAT'S THIS ALL ABOUT, THEN?' BIT

I wanted to start this book with a quote. Mr Keegan, who's my headteacher and takes us for history on Friday afternoons, says our essays should start with a quote that sets up what it's going to be about.

I wanted to write about brilliant female scientists, and you know what? There aren't any. Not brilliant female scientists; there are plenty of those – not that anyone ever knows any. Except Marie Curie, maybe. I've read all about her. There aren't any *quotes* about brilliant female scientists, I mean.

Cos this story's totally about them. You're going to love it.

So instead, I'm going to use:

If you give up, it means you never really wanted it in the first place.

Said by my Granny Joss. My dad's mum.

Cos this story's all about her too. My granny's a brilliant female scientist, you see, except I didn't know anything about it, at first. And this story's all about our determination to succeed, even when it seemed like the whole world was against us. And this story's about me. *Je m'appelle* Matilda Moore. *J'ai douze ans*. That's French. You're going to need that later. I am twelve and I am from Arnos Yarm, which is a boring old village in Canterbury, and I am an inventor. Nice to meet you.

Welcome to the tale of my outrageous, electrifying, marvellicifous (I made up that word – I told you I'm an inventor) couple of days with my Granny Joss.

For, within one thirty-one-hour period, we had:

- Escaped from an old people's care home in a laundry basket
- Rescued a drowning man from the English Channel
- Flown a hot-air balloon across Paris
- Become friends with Europe's most wanted criminal
- Tended to a poisoned lion
- Gate-crashed the Nobel Prize ceremony in Sweden

It's exhausting just reading about it, isn't it? You'd better hang onto your hats, all of you who are wearing one. And if you're not wearing one, hold onto your hair. And if you're bald, not a problem, grab a tea towel.

We'd better start at the beginning.

1

THE HANDY-
HANDY-HAND

You're meant to describe yourself in books, so here goes:

I'm short for my age. I have light brown shoulder-length hair that I never brush because I have more important things on my mind like, 'What shall I create today?' to be worrying about how I look. I always wear blue dungarees because they have the most pockets, and I have a pencil tucked behind my ear, a tape measure somewhere about my person and a sketchbook in my rucksack. I AM READY TO INVENT AT ALL TIMES!

I *look* like I'd fall over and snap in a heavy wind. I *look* like I should be painting my nails or watching *Keeping Up With The Kardashians* like most of my classmates. But I like surprising people. I like the look on their faces when I tell them I'm an inventor. As if girls shouldn't do that.

A famous guy called Thomas Edison once said, *To invent, you need a good imagination, and a pile of junk.* He was the chap who invented the light bulb, so he was a bright spark. (That had better not be a pity laugh, you guys.)

I have both – a good imagination and tons of *stuff*. Admittedly, not all of it mine. My parents are forever saying things like, 'Matilda, HOW MANY TIMES have I told you NOT to dismantle the bookcase to use for your woodwork?' And, 'WHO has taken my brand-new pair of shoelaces? They were right here!' while looking directly at *me*.

My idols in life are:

- ISAMBARD KINGDOM BRUNEL. He built huge bridges, like the Clifton Suspension Bridge, huge ships, like the SS Great Britain, huge train stations, like London Paddington, and probably also some stuff that was small, like maybe a loo-roll holder. (I don't know that for certain.)

- EMILY CUMMINS. She was only a teenager when she invented a fridge that refrigerates itself. As in, you haven't got to plug it into anything in order for food to stay cool inside it, which helps people in places that don't have a lot of plugs.
- MARY ANDERSON. You know when it's raining and your dad's driving and puts the windscreen wipers on? Thank you, Mary Anderson. (She invented the wipers.)

There are loads more – I'm going to create a whole list of them at the end of the book, you lucky things.

I've wanted to be an inventor for as long as I can remember. Aged four, I decided to modify the toaster to make a better play-space for my hamster. All I'll say about it is that we weren't allowed another toaster in the house after that. Or a hamster.

So far, in my twelve years on this earth, I have invented:

- The Tinsel Twizzler! Does your dad make you use the same Christmas decorations every year? Are the strips of tinsel tangled up in knots in the box? Simply press a button on this modified tape measure and watch the decorations curl into a neat round coil.

· The Garden Grabber! Kicked a ball over your neighbour's fence for the millionth time? Simply fish it out with this long curtain pole with a modified claw attached and you'll never have to sheepishly ring their doorbell again!

· The Tickle Trouncer! Fed up with annoying relatives tickling you every time they come to visit? Simply wear this vest modified from pillowcases and your mum's best cushions (sorry about that, Mum) and be immune to their clutches! (And also extraceedingly warm.)

My Grandad Wilf was my mentor. Once a week, my parents and I would visit him and Granny Joss for Sunday lunch. I knew that Granny Joss had been a scientist herself, years and years ago, but she didn't talk about it *at all* and I wasn't allowed to ask her about it. Dad said she'd left the profession 'under a cloud', which I didn't really understand and think has something to do with rain. Grandad Wilf was a vet before he retired, but he was an inventor in his spare time, so he and I would leave my parents and Granny Joss drinking boring cups of tea and disappear into his workshop at the bottom of the garden and invent like mad. It was my very best favourite hour of the week.

The reason I love inventing so much? Because *anything is possible*! You start with a blank page and no clue what you're going to sketch. And then an idea whizz-pops into your mind and you think, 'Ooh, what if I could invent a way to scoop toast out of the toaster *without* totally burning my fingers?' and you outline a diagram and then you work out how to build it and you cut metal or sand wood and build, build, build, and then you have the finished product that *you have totally made from your imagination*!

Grandad Wilf also taught me the saying, *Necessity is the mother of invention*. It means that most inventions are created to fix a problem. Like Emily Cummins, helping people with their fridge situation.

Which brings us to my greatest invention yet: The Handy-Handy-Hand.

Grandad Wilf's hands didn't work as well as they used to. His fingers were gnarled and he found it difficult to hold his tools. 'Arthritis,' Granny Joss said. I knew how much this got him down, and so, ladies and gentlemen, without further ado, it's my great pleasure to introduce you to The Handy-Handy-Hand!

A wooden glove, with interchangeable metal fingers that would do the work Grandad Wilf's hands couldn't! Need to shave? No problem! Swap the 'fork' finger for the 'razor blade', press a button on the palm, and away you go. Can't peel an orange for a delicious and nutritious snack? Chill out! Swap the 'scraping earwax' finger for a 'mini penknife' and peel that pith away!

I built it all by myself. Grandad Wilf loved it, and he helped me get a UK patent for it too, which means that we filed my invention with the government and if anyone tries to copy it and claim The Handy-Handy-Hand was their idea, I can say: *Well, you can jog on!*

Grandad Wilf died a few months after that, and it was like the world was suddenly greyer. I'd wake up in the middle of the night with an idea ('What if you could invent a machine that *automatically* opens a brand-new loo roll, so that you don't keep shredding the paper when you try to open it?') and I'd think, 'Oh, just *wait* until Grandad Wilf hears this one!' and it would hit me three seconds later that he was gone and I couldn't tell him anything.

Granny Joss gave me everything from Grandad's workshop, because not only was I the rightful heir to his tools, but she was packing up to move into a care home down the road. She didn't want to live in a house all alone and one that held so many memories of her life with Grandad.

My parents and I continued to visit Granny Joss, but it wasn't the same. Grandad Wilf wasn't there. The workshop wasn't there. There was no one for me to talk to about inventions. Dad's an accountant. The only thing he's ever invented is a way of typing 'EGGSHELL' on his calculator. (Press 77345993 and hold it upside down. See? Riveting.) Mum's an office manager. She spends her days ordering stationery and filing expenses. Not much fun there, either. Granny Joss used to do sciencey things with space and the planets, but like I said, that was a *no-go zone*.

Instead, these weekly visits to the care home would consist of helping Granny Joss complete a jigsaw puzzle and listening to classical music.

Life without Grandad Wilf and his enthusiasm for inventions was very much duller.

Then one day, not long ago, my school announced they'd be holding a science competition, with a Grand Prize for the best invention or scientific display. There was a poster put up on the noticeboard and everything:

**Think you're the next Albert Einstein?
Got an invention or a science trick that's
better than sliced bread? Want to win a
GRAND PRIZE? Arnos Yarm
Comprehensive's Science Competition
is the chance to show the world
(well, Arnos Yarm)
what you're made of!**

Ask your form teacher for details.

Well, I would! I *would* ask my form teacher for details! Because I knew *exactly* what invention I was going to enter. And sorry, any of you suckers hoping for the Grand Prize, cos it was mine!

At least it was until Thomas Thomas came along.

2

THOMAS THOMAS

With absolutely no consideration of how it would affect his chances in life, Mr and Mrs Thomas had decided to call their son, their only child, Thomas. Thomas Thomas. As if there wasn't anything else in the whole world they could have called him instead. Names that would have been better for Thomas Thomas than Thomas Thomas:

- Timothy Thomas
- Republic of Ireland Thomas
- Republic of the Congo Thomas
- The Galactic Republic from Star Wars Thomas
- Sarah Thomas
- Anything Other Than Thomas Thomas. (And that's not me saying 'Just call him anything other than Thomas.' It's me

13

saying, 'Even if his name was Anything Other Than Thomas Thomas, that would still be a squillion times better.')

I hope, dear reader, that after mocking the name, none of you reading this is called Thomas Thomas. If you are, I'm sorry.

I'm sorry that your name is Thomas Thomas.

As well as having a silly name, Thomas Thomas sat next to me in science and *always* had to copy my answers, which was just plain old cheating. He was *not* the sort of boy who should win the Grand Prize at the science competition.

The competition took place on a Friday afternoon in December. Every single pupil was packed into the hall, like it was Morning Assembly, because it meant time off lessons. I spied four other pupils in the crowd with their scientific displays tucked under their arm, just like me with The Handy-Handy-Hand. I had half a mind to tell them not to bother wasting their time, but everyone was always banging on about 'Team Spirit' at this school, so I figured I'd better not.

At two o'clock, Mr Keegan stepped on stage. 'Welcome, one and all,' he boomed, 'to Arnos Yarm's inaugural Science Competition. Would all those taking part come up here with your efforts, please.'

In my head, I practised my winner's speech. I would dedicate the award to Grandad Wilf, of course. But would it be too much to thank Leonardo da Vinci too? Or Tim Berners-Lee?

One by one, Mr Keegan called the contestants to the front of the stage to show off what they'd brought. A scruffy-looking boy named Josh went first. He held a glass of water in one hand and an egg in the other. 'See this glass?' he said, lifting it up for the crowd to see. 'See this egg?' But his hand must have been sweaty, because the egg fell right out of it, and landed with a SPLAT! on Mr Keegan's brown shoes.

Our headteacher shook his leg furiously. Speckles of raw egg were flung out over the crowd. 'I guess that's a forfeit then,' Mr Keegan huffed and moved to the next contestant.

'Wait!' Josh cried. 'My trick!'

Mr Keegan glared at him. His shoes were ruined. 'If you're attempting to show that an egg can float in a glass of water if you've added salt to it, then I'm afraid,' he sighed, 'the trick is useless *without* the egg. You've simply got a glass of water.'

I smiled to myself. This was going to be a piece of cake.

Next up was Thomas Thomas. He picked up a huge bottle of Coke from the floor beside him. He fumbled in his pocket for his wallet and held that up to the crowd. 'Ladies and gentlemen,' he cried. 'Behold the scientific trick of ero – erodnee – eros . . .' He looked about him, confused.

'Eroding,' I whispered. I'd seen this science trick on the internet.

'Eroding money!' Thomas Thomas eventually declared.

With that, he unscrewed the lid of the Coke bottle and guzzled the whole lot. HE GUZZLED IT! The whole lot! He poured it down his gullet like nobody's business! Two whole litres' worth!

And then, understandably, he gave an almighty BELCH – a loud BEEEUUURRRGGHHH! blasting from his belly. Thomas Thomas, looking ever so pleased with himself, as well as ever so sick, opened his wallet and took a five-pound note from it, which he stuffed inside the now-empty Coke bottle. 'Alacazam!' he cried.

Nobody said anything. The crowd looked to one another, not sure what they'd just witnessed.

'If you're trying to do what I *think* you're trying to do,' I said, actually starting to feel sorry for the moron, 'you're meant to drop a penny into a bottle of Coke. The phosphoric acid in the drink reacts with the copper of the coin and dissolves it. *That's* eroding money. And it's not magic, it's science.'

Thomas Thomas looked from me to the five-pound note in the empty bottle. 'Same thing,' he shrugged. I mean, honestly!

Then, after a Year 8 girl had used a hairdryer to blow some ping-pong balls into the air, and a girl in Year 10 had produced a papier-mâché volcano, complete with exploding lava bubbling over the top, which wasn't half bad, it was *finally* my turn. Time to give everyone something to get excited about.

True enough, the audience clapped in appreciation as I put the glove on Mr Keegan's left hand and showed off all the different functions it could be used for. There were audible gasps of delight and amazement!

I imagined this is how it felt when John Logie Baird first gave the world television. It was so obvious who the winner would be.

After we had all presented our efforts, three men walked on stage. They all looked like each other – tweed jacket, big round belly and just a few strands of hair combed over their shiny bald heads. 'Let's hear it for our local councillors,' Mr Keegan said, gesturing to the men. 'Mr Varney, Mr Dorfman and Mr Yonker.'

Everyone clapped politely. 'I'm delighted to be here today,' Mr Yonker said, taking charge, 'and to present the Grand Prize of one thousand pounds!'

I let out a gasp of amazement. One thousand pounds? I ran through all the things I could buy with that:

A Black & Decker drill.

A workbench.

A new tool box.

'One thousand pounds,' Mr Yonker repeated, before adding, extraceedingly quietly, 'of Varney Yonker Dorfman Quality Dog Food Vouchers.'

'What?' I said, just catching the end of his sentence. '*Dog food* vouchers?'

'The winner,' Mr Yonker ploughed on, ignoring me, 'of Arnos Yarm Comprehensive's Grand Science Prize is . . .'

I held my breath and crossed my fingers. I don't know why I was so nervous. This was mine!

'Thomas Thomas!' Mr Yonker cried.

'WHAT?' I yelled. That couldn't be right!

'Thomas Thomas?' I repeated. 'THOMAS THOMAS? A boy so stupid he *drank* his experiment away?'

'Now, now,' Mr Keegan said, trying to hustle me off the stage. Thomas Thomas stepped forward to shake hands with the three councillors and smiled for the school photographer, his stupid grin plastered over his stupid face.

This was outrageous. 'What about The Handy-Handy-Hand?' I cried. 'That's better than all of them!'

Mr Yonker stopped smiling for photos and peered down on me. 'We've made our decision,' he stated.

'But The Handy-Handy-Hand's the best!' I yelled. 'It's got a UK patent and everything!'

Mr Varney sighed. 'We've awarded the prize to someone who clearly didn't cheat,' he declared.

'Thomas Thomas may not have got the experiment right, but at least he did it all by himself.'

'I didn't cheat—' I protested, but I was shoved out of the way by the other contestants rushing to look at Thomas Thomas's dog food vouchers. 'I made it for my grandad,' I said.

'You're just a little girl,' Mr Dorfman scoffed. 'I highly doubt you did. The invention required welding and soldering and—'

'And drilling and cutting metal,' I butted in. 'I did all of that in my grandad's workshop! By myself!'

But Mr Dorfman, Mr Varney and Mr Yonker didn't care. They clearly thought I was lying. Everyone did. Nobody thought I was capable of inventing and building The Handy-Handy-Hand just because I was a girl.

And it was this, the sheer *injustice* of it all – the fact that someone far less deserving should win the Grand Prize – that kicked everything off.

And it's where this story *really*, totally, I've-said-it-before-and-I'll-say-it-again-hold-onto-your-hats-people-this-is-the-real-deal *really* takes off. Ready?

3

INJUSTICE IS A MAN CALLED SMOCKS

'It's not fair!' is a cry heard in homes all over the world. Normally, mums and dads roll their eyes and say annoying grown-up things, like, 'Life's not fair. Get used to it!' But this time, it really *wasn't* fair!

Why should Thomas Thomas, a boy so stupid he was named twice, by a mum and dad so stupid they couldn't think of ANY OTHER NAME to call him, win? *My* invention was the best!

All right, I wasn't *particularly* fussed about the vouchers – we didn't have a dog, after all. But it was the glory! It was the fact that I *should* have been crowned the winner!

As I trudged off stage, The Handy-Handy-Hand tucked under my arm, I wiped my eyes with the sleeve of my blazer. I didn't want anyone knowing how upset I was.

The home-time bell couldn't come quickly enough. All I wanted was to crawl into bed and hide under the duvet for the entire weekend, but I had to sit through a boring lesson on 'The Path of the River Thames' first. And when I eventually traipsed through the school gates at 3.30 p.m. I spotted my parents parked up in the car outside, the last of the day's sun glinting off the car's freshly-buffed roof. My dad was extraceedingly car-proud. He washed and waxed the car to within an inch of its shiny-black life twice a week. He would spray Febreze and hoover inside after *every* single journey. He wore white leather driving gloves so he wouldn't leave smears on the steering wheel. He even called the car 'Her Majesty' in private, without realizing Mum and I knew about the nickname.

Dad grinned at me and held up a plate of cakes triple-wrapped for safety in clingfilm. Crumbs inside the car were a definite no-no. 'Something for your granny,' he explained. 'We've got to pop to the home to sign some forms and it was two-for-one on lemon drizzle at Sainsbury's. It's not a Saturday Big Shop

Treat, I know, but I thought we'd live a little. Fancy a slice?'

Granny Joss's care home was located in a quiet, leafy street three roads from my school and seven streets from my house. Arnos Yarm wasn't very big, to be honest.

When we got there, the TV in the lounge was blaring out a news item about a British professor who was to be awarded a grand prize in two days' time for something or other. Every resident but Granny Joss was gathered round the TV. She sat on her own in an armchair at the back of the room, looking thoroughly miserable. I didn't blame her for not joining in. I'd had enough of grand prizes myself.

'Oh, marvellous,' Dad said sarcastically, plonking the plate of cakes down on the coffee table. 'Two moody Moores. That's all we need.'

I frowned. I'd told my parents what had happened at the science competition as we'd driven to the home, but they didn't seem to be taking it very seriously.

'Why?' Granny Joss asked. She patted my knee softly. 'What's up with you, dearie?'

Granny Joss had lived in Canterbury for the last thirty years, but she'd been born and raised in Scotland and even now, at the age of eighty, still had the traces of a Scottish accent. She was a typical, average granny. She was tall and thin and had a shock of frizzy white hair. She liked jigsaw puzzles and tea and classical music. She wore hiking boots, as if she was ready to dash for the hills at a moment's notice, which was ridiculous seeing as she'd never left Arnos Yarm in all the time I'd been alive.

'I don't want to talk about it,' I mumbled. I reached into my pocket and pulled out my mobile. It wasn't a fancy one – there weren't any games or apps on it – but I wanted to avoid her stare.

'Matilda's a little disappointed,' Dad whispered to Granny Joss.

'Oh?' she replied, her voice full of concern.

Nobody said anything for a moment. The sound from the TV filled the silence. It was still banging on about that professor and his award.

'Another boy won the science prize at school,' Mum piped up eventually.

I knew Mum was merely explaining to Granny what had happened, but there was *more* to my disappointment than that! 'Yeah, and he *shouldn't* have done,' I yelled hotly.

Granny Joss's eyebrows shot up. Some of the other residents turned to stare at me in shock.

'Forget it,' I muttered. 'You wouldn't understand.' I looked down at the ground. '*Grandad* would have.'

Grandad Wilf had been the only one in my family who *truly* understood why I loved inventing. He'd been so creative and full of ideas, like me. My parents were extraceedingly sensible people who never did anything out of the ordinary. Dad, being an accountant, often wore a suit, even at weekends. He had his hair trimmed neatly once a month at the same barber. His ties were always grey – never anything so fancy as salmon pink or dusty yellow. Mum was the same. She wore long skirts and cardigans and practical shoes and liked programmes about needlework. My parents encouraged my enthusiasm for science and engineering and they applauded my passion, but I think they thought I was a bit nuts, thinking up all sorts of weird and wacky things to invent.

My chest tightened, thinking about Grandad Wilf. He would have understood *everything*. He would have jumped up on stage and shouted, 'GIVE MY GRANDDAUGHTER THE PRIZE SHE DESERVES, YONKER!'

Dad and Granny Joss shared a look. Mum munched on her cake. Moments ticked by. I could feel Granny Joss's eyes searching my face, debating what to do.

All of a sudden, she jumped to her feet – rather impressively for an eighty-year-old. 'Come with me,' she said, holding out her hand.

'I haven't done anything!' I protested.

'You're not in trouble. I want to show you something.' She heaved me to my feet and led me from the common room, through the hall and up the stairs.

'Where are we going?' I asked. I'd never been upstairs before. We always stayed in the lounge when we visited. I took in the faded swirling carpet of the hall, the framed pictures of birds in the stairwell.

Granny Joss walked to the bay window at the end of the second-floor landing. There was a flowery armchair positioned in front of it, with a brass telescope next to that. Granny Joss put her eye to the telescope and fiddled around with a couple of knobs. 'Almost there,' she said. 'Just a few more degrees to the left ...' She sighed. 'Marjory's been playing around with this again. This is mine – a rather *special* telescope – I did have it all set up.'

'To what?' I asked. I hovered directly behind Granny Joss, trying to see what she could.

'There!' Granny Joss exclaimed, after a moment. 'Look.'

She moved aside and I bent down and stared through the eyepiece. The night had drawn in and millions of stars dotted the sky, all twinkling back at me, like a carpet of black with grains of sugar scattered over it. 'What am I looking for?' I asked.

'The known universe is made up of ten billion galaxies,' Granny Joss said. I couldn't help but note the excitement creeping into her voice. She'd never sounded like this before. 'Assuming there is an average of one hundred billion stars per galaxy – it varies, you see – that means there are approximately one billion trillion stars in the observable universe.'

'Riiiight,' I said, continuing to peer through the telescope. 'So . . .?'

'Can you see one star shining brighter than all the others?' Granny Joss asked. She hopped from one foot to the other behind me.

I squinted my eyes and wiggled the telescope around until, eventually, one star shone out above all else. 'I see it!' I cried. 'Right there. Why's it so bright?'

'Because it's a planet, not a star,' Granny Joss replied. 'It's millions and millions of light years away. It's bright because it's bigger than even all the stars in its cluster.'

'Is it Neptune or something?' I asked.

Granny Joss shook her head. 'You're not even looking at *our* solar system. This is a planet further out in the Milky Way.'

As much as this was taking my mind from what had happened at school earlier, I couldn't work out what she was getting at. 'And?' I said.

'It's called Planet Smocks,' Granny Joss said, more quietly this time. She let out a long sigh. 'Named after the man on the news this evening. The one being awarded the prize for discovering it.'

'And . . .?' I repeated. I was starting to get tired now. It had been a long day. A long, disappointing day.

'And,' Granny Joss said, in a smaller voice than ever, 'it shouldn't have been named after Professor Smocks, because Professor Smocks did *not* discover it.'

I frowned. 'But if he didn't discover the planet, who did? Who *should* it be named after?'

Granny Joss sighed once more. 'Me,' she said. 'It was me.'

4

I THINK GRANNY'S
GONE MAD

I stared at Granny Joss. I wasn't entirely convinced I'd heard her correctly. 'Sorry, *what*?'

Granny Joss slumped into the armchair. 'I'm an astrophysicist,' she declared, as if that explained everything. 'At least I was, once. Not long after I married your grandad – crikey, this is going back a good fifty years – we moved to London so I could research radio waves emitting from stars. Professor Smocks was my boss at the Royal Observatory in Greenwich.'

'Sorry, *what*?' I repeated. I knew Granny Joss had worked in science, but I'd always imagined she'd collected up the test tubes in the lab or something. 'You discovered that planet?'

'I did,' Granny Joss nodded. 'Except I didn't know what it was at the time.' She cleared her throat and gazed out of the window, casting her mind back. 'I'd been examining the radio waves from a particular cluster of stars in another solar system and, late one night, I discovered XT28E. It was a star that didn't behave like all the other stars around it. I showed it to Professor Smocks the next morning, but he didn't think there was anything to it. I thought there might be, that perhaps it was *more* than a star, but this was the 1960s – the technology to travel that far into space to investigate hadn't been invented yet. I believed that one day it *would* be possible for a space probe to go the distance, so I did the maths and charted the probe's course and I came up with the equation that would make it achievable. I showed all my work to Smocks, who seemed more interested this time and said he would double-check everything, and then the next thing I knew, it was all over the news that *he* had discovered the star.'

'That's not fair!' I cried.

Granny Joss shook her head. 'No,' she said. 'It's not. Professor Smocks stole my work, but he was more senior than me and people respected him. There weren't many female scientists around back then, hardly any. No one had any reason to think that Professor Smocks *hadn't* made the discovery.' I detected a tear well up in her eyes, but she quickly coughed to cover it up.

'What about the planet part?' I asked. 'How come it's now Planet Smocks?'

'Because only in the last decade has the technology capable of travelling to the star been invented,' Granny Joss explained. 'NASA launched a probe seven years ago, using *my* equation, and when it finally got near XT28E last year, they discovered it was indeed not a star in a binary system as they had thought, but an actual planet. Smocks has spent the last fifty years telling the world it was *his* work, hence why NASA named the planet after him.'

I couldn't believe it. How had I never known this about Granny Joss? 'Dad always says,' I hesitated, not quite sure how to put it, 'that you left the science profession under a cloud. Was it because of this?'

Granny Joss looked downcast. Her piercing blue eyes weren't as twinkly as they'd been a moment ago. 'That's right,' she replied. 'I protested to the Observatory,

but they just thought I was jealous of Smocks. I realized I couldn't stay there any longer.'

Well, I wasn't having this. How *dare* Professor
Smocks steal from my granny! How *dare* he claim
the credit – and a prize – for all her work! This was
far, far worse than Thomas Thomas copying my
answers in science *and* me not winning the Grand
Prize because I'm a girl.

I could feel the anger rise within me. *Two days*, the
news report had said. Professor Smocks was to be
awarded his grand prize in two days. Which meant
we still had time. 'We have to tell the world it was
you!' I said. 'Come on!' I helped Granny Joss to her
feet and led her back downstairs.

'Granny Joss is a famous scientist!' I cried as we
burst into the lounge. 'But some evil dude stole her
discovery.'

Every single person in the lounge turned to stare at
my outburst, but I didn't care. This was *far* too important.

Dad let out a puff of air. 'I knew this would come up,'
he muttered to himself. 'As soon as I saw that news item.'

'Keep your voice down, love,' Mum whispered.
'You're creating a scene.'

'Good!' I said. 'I want to! I want to tell the whole world about this – this *injustice*!' There was that word again. What was it with the Moore family being denied our scientific glory?

Dad and Granny Joss shared a look. 'It's too late, sweetheart,' Dad stated calmly to me. 'Professor Smocks is to be awarded the Nobel Prize in Physics this Sunday.'

'WHAT?!?' I cried. '*That's* the grand prize?' I knew what a Nobel Prize was. It was a very famous global award, given each year to the person who had most contributed to their field. It wasn't just a prize given to people in Physics, either – there was a Nobel Prize in Chemistry, Literature, Economics, Medicine and Peace too.

And trust me, it was a heck of a lot better than one thousand pounds' worth of Varney Yonker Dorfman Quality Dog Food Vouchers, and I'd been annoyed I hadn't even won *that*.

I raced to the TV and, changing the channel from a glamorous woman solving a maths puzzle back to the news, turned up the volume. There was a picture of Professor Smocks plastered all over the screen. It wasn't a recent picture either, by the looks of it, because by Granny Joss's reckoning, Professor Smocks should be in his eighties too, like her. Instead, he looked at least forty years younger, in what he obviously thought was the prime of his life. He had silky blond hair, round tortoiseshell glasses, a purple velvet suit and the most annoying smug smile I'd ever seen.

'Professor Smocks is getting the Nobel Prize in Physics on Sunday in honour of *your* discovery fifty years ago!' I yelled.

The residents whispered excitedly to each other. This was more dramatic than *Countdown*!

'We have to stop him,' I said. 'Where is it, this prize ceremony?' Arnos Yarm wasn't far from London, and that's where most big events happened – Trooping the Colour, the Olympics, Taylor Swift at the O2. We could probably catch the train. Or Dad could drive. We could be there in an hour, probably.

'Sweden,' Granny Joss replied. 'Stockholm City Hall, to be exact.'

Right. Just *slightly* further than London, then. 'O-kaaay,' I said, my mind whirring like the clappers.

35

'We could see if there's a last-minute flight? Or a train? Or a ferry?'

'It's a very long way to go, love,' Mum said, shaking her head.

My parents had never had a sense of adventure. We hadn't ever even gone on holiday outside the UK, because they said there was plenty to see on our own doorstep – we didn't need aeroplanes. Even though I'd explained to them a *thousand* times how aeroplanes were one of the best inventions of the last one hundred years.

'But it's the right thing to do,' I replied.

Dad nodded. 'It is. And we *should* do something.'

'Yesssssssss!' Now they were talking! I grabbed my rucksack and slung it on my shoulders. 'I'll check flight times.'

Dad held up his hand to stop me. 'No!' he stated. 'We're not going anywhere. We'll do things the official way. From home.'

'What?'

'Your granny tried to sort all this out in 1967,' Dad said calmly, 'but no one listened. I'm not gallivanting halfway across the world in the hope that people listen now. But if you want, we'll start a petition. I'll write an official letter of complaint to the Nobel Prize board. I'll explain everything. But we'll go through the proper channels.'

'We could write to the Prime Minister,' Mum chipped in, her eyes bright with excitement. It was one of the most creative suggestions she'd ever made.

A petition? A letter? 'That won't be enough,' I replied. I knew Dad meant well, but the ceremony was *this Sunday*. 'The letter won't even get there in time. We have to go to Sweden and explain to the judges and all the board members that the prize is really Granny's, before Smocks gets his hands on it. That's the only thing to do.'

'Now, look here, Matilda,' Dad said in a stern tone. He put down his tea cup. Things had got serious. 'Your granny's eighty. Her legs don't work like they used to. She can't do long journeys. She gets tired easily. Her passport expired in 1993—'

'My legs are perfectly fine, thank you very much,' Granny Joss interrupted crossly.

'Eighty's not *that* old,' the two ladies in the armchairs next to us piped up in solidarity.

'Let's all just calm down,' Dad said. 'It's great that you want to help your granny, Matilda, but I don't want you getting Mum's hopes up. Professor Smocks has been dining out on "his" discovery for years. The whole world thinks he was behind it. It'll be really hard to convince everyone he wasn't.' He looked at Granny Joss. 'Especially when there's no proof Mum was even involved. Not any more.'

'What does that mean?' I asked.

Granny Joss let out a deep sigh. 'I threw away all my paperwork and photographs years ago, when I realized no one would ever believe me. I didn't want to be reminded of all the years of frustration and heartache.'

'Didn't you patent the planet,' I asked, 'so no one could copy it? Like I did with The Handy-Handy-Hand?'

Granny Joss shook her head softly.

I hated seeing her this miserable. 'Well, who cares about proof?' I said. 'We have the truth on our side!'

Dad frowned, but he didn't say anything else. I couldn't believe everyone could be so calm about this. Why weren't we heading for the airport immediately? I mean, I didn't have a passport, what with never having been abroad before, but that wasn't the point. We *had* to get to Sweden somehow. Why couldn't Mum and Dad see that?

Mum looked around at all of us brightly. 'What a day!' she said in a forced cheery voice. 'I think it's high time we all thought about bed. We can start the petition in the morning.'

I don't think my parents *quite* understood how urgent this was.

But I knew better than to argue with them. They clearly weren't going to budge. It would have to be up to me to save the day.

'Fine,' I said, as sweetly as I could muster. 'Why don't I escort you upstairs, Granny Joss?'

Dad's eyebrows shot up in surprise at my change of heart. But, as Grandad Wilf used to say, 'Necessity is the mother of invention, Matilda.'

And this time, I'd need to be more inventive than ever.

5

WAYS TO ESCAPE FROM
A CARE HOME

'Lovely,' Dad said, beaming at me. He was clearly glad all this 'let's storm the Nobel Prize ceremony' nonsense was over with. 'I'll get thinking about what to write to the Prime Minister. How about that?'

I took Granny Joss by the arm, and for the second time that evening we walked up the faded stairs of the care home and along the flowery-wallpapered landing. I glanced at the telescope by the window. Seeing it again made me even more determined.

As we reached Granny Joss's bedroom door, I squeezed her hand. 'Granny,' I said, my voice all serious and calm. 'We *have* to get you to Sweden. We *have* to burst into the Nobel Prize ceremony and say, "STOP WHAT YOU'RE DOING! THAT MAN

IS A FRAUD!" and I'll point to Professor Smocks and tell the whole world that he's stolen your planet and that *you* should win the Grand Science Prize, whether it's dog food vouchers or not.'

Granny Joss didn't know what I was talking about dog food vouchers for, but she smiled at me anyway. 'Your parents are right, Matilda,' she said. 'I don't have a passport. And I don't know why anyone would listen to me now.'

'Because we'll *make* them.' I grinned at her. 'We'll *make* the judges listen.' I leaned in, conspiratorial-like. 'And here's how we'll get you there. I'll take a white coat from the dinner lady in the kitchen and dress you as a doctor so you can waltz out the front door. Then you steal the care home minibus and drive us all the way to Sweden. And when the people at passport control ask for our passports, we say, "This is a medical emergency. I haven't got time for your ridiculous questioning."'

Granny Joss's piercing blue eyes twinkled at the suggestion.

Another thought flashed into my head. 'I've got it! You hide under the Meals on Wheels trolley and wheel yourself all the way to Stockholm and you bribe the border officials with chicken and mushroom hotpots. What do you reckon?'

Granny Joss chuckled as I relayed all this to her. I joined in too – it was the first time I'd laughed all evening. It didn't make losing to Thomas Thomas and finding out about Granny Joss's injustice any easier, but it felt nice to share a giggle with her.

Granny Joss planted a kiss on my cheek. 'You're a good girl,' she said. 'Your grandad would be proud. Like I am. But I only told you about Professor Smocks so that you'd know I understand. I'm not your grandad, but I do know what you're going through.' Tears welled up in her eyes. 'We'll write a letter and start a petition and see what happens, all right? I think that's all we can do. Night-night, love.' She shot me a watery smile, and then stepped inside her bedroom and closed the door.

I frowned at the 'ROOM 17: JOSS MOORE' name plaque staring back at me, willing Granny Joss to open the door again, suitcase packed, ready to go, shouting, 'You're absolutely right, granddaughter of mine! Of course we have to gate-crash the

Nobel Prize ceremony and scream, "PROFESSOR SMOCKS! YOU, SIR, ARE A CHARLATAN! A CHARLATAN, I TELL YOU! GOOD DAY TO YOU!" and I'll claim my rightful glory! And it'll show all the stupid Thomas Thomases of this world what's what!'

But Granny Joss didn't.

So I let out a long sigh and went back downstairs.

6

THE SEED HAS BEEN
PLANTED

I find it hard to sleep at the best of times, with so many thoughts swirling around my mind. And although I must have dozed off for a bit, it was still dark when I woke up again – woke up with what felt like a network of pylons inside my head, lighting up my brain like Battersea Power Station. I knew we had to get justice for Granny Joss. Mum and Dad might not believe that going to Sweden was the right thing to do, but I did. We *had* to confront Professor Smocks about what he'd done. The lack of proof and passports, though; that was tricky.

I listened for any noise from my parents' bedroom, but all was quiet throughout the house, so I crept downstairs and switched on the computer in the dining room. The first thing that came up when I typed in 'Professor Smocks' was his website. A different photo from the news broadcast stared out at me, one where Smocks was in a white coat and held up a glass rectangular plate with lots of black spots dotted across it. He was still grinning his smug smile in this one, though.

Next to Professor Smocks's name was a long list of letters, which stood for his various qualifications. I knew all about that. Dad was 'Malcolm Moore FCA CTA', which meant he was a qualified accountant. Here, Professor Smocks was:

Professor Doctor Tarquin Neville Ignatius Smocks BSc MPhys PhD Gold Blue Peter Badge.

Tarquin Neville Ignatius. What a ridiculous name!

It wasn't enough to cheer me up. I carried on scrolling through pages and pages of searches. They were all articles about 'Smocks's great discovery' and nearly all of them had a picture of him with that glass plate. There was no hint of Granny Joss in any of them. There was no hint of anything that looked like proof.

That's what made me write to the Prime Minister, after all. Maybe she'd be able to get to the bottom of what really happened. She could get MI5 on it! I found the email address on the government website and wrote this:

Dear Prime Minister

I hope this email finds you well. My dad always puts that in business emails to clients and I want you to know this is an email about a serious business. It's about a theft of scientific research. I tried to find a quote about that to start off the email like Mr Keegan says we should, but guess what? There aren't any. So all I will say is this:

PROFESSOR DOCTOR TARQUIN NEVILLE IGNATIUS SMOCKS BSC MPHYS PHD GOLD BLUE PETER BADGE STOLE MY GRANNY'S RESEARCH ON A BRAND-NEW STAR SHE DISCOVERED BACK IN 1967, WHICH TURNED OUT TO BE A PLANET ACTUALLY, AND ON SUNDAY HE IS TO BE AWARDED THE NOBEL PRIZE IN PHYSICS FOR IT.

I wrote that all in capitals, because I told you it is a serious business.

My granny is called Professor Joss Moore and she discovered the planet really, but because she is a woman no one believed her. And you are a woman and I hope you do.

Please can you make sure that Professor Smocks isn't given the award and that my granny is instead? And maybe the Gold Blue Peter Badge too, while we're at it? That would be nice.

Thanks! I didn't vote for you, I'm only twelve, but if you're still around when I can vote in six years' time, I might.

Matilda Moore, aged 12

Inventor (The Handy-Handy-Hand mainly, but I'm working on other stuff)

Also – my mum and dad are going to write to you too, but their letter won't be half as interestingly brilliant as mine. (But they still mean well.)

As soon as I pressed 'SEND', a new email pinged into my inbox. The subject heading said 'AUTO RESPONSE: 10 DOWNING STREET' and the email stated:

Thank you for your recent email to the Prime Minister's Office. All emails are read and we will do our best to ensure you receive a response within one month.

One month? That *couldn't* be our best hope, could it? I let out a sigh. Without actual proof, maybe yes. Maybe Mum and Dad were right.

I scrolled through the pages of internet searches again, just in case I'd missed anything. But it was all Professor Smocks and his stupid face and his stupid smugness and his stupid glass plate. My eyelids drooped. I checked the time on the computer – 03.07 a.m. Oh, if *only* Granny Joss hadn't thrown out all her paperwork. If only—

A thought whizz-popped into my head.

The glass plate with the black splodges all over it. I'd seen it before, of course I had! And not just on the ten pages of internet searches I'd scrolled through again and again for the past hour. When Granny Joss had given me the contents of Grandad Wilf's workshop, there had been among them a tatty cardboard box, filled with boring old bits of paperwork and a rectangular glass plate covered in black smudges and spots. I thought Granny Joss had obviously given me this by mistake, but I hadn't said anything about that, cos I hadn't wanted to make her even more upset.

Now I switched off the computer and ran back upstairs, taking them two at a time. I burst into my bedroom and rummaged under my bed. I pulled out the tatty cardboard box and plucked out the rectangular glass plate. It was *exactly* the same one Professor Smocks held in the photos of him, except this one had the initials 'J. M.' at the bottom, alongside a date. I peered at the black splodges more closely. They were dotted all over the plate, but there was a cluster of five spots right in the middle, with one splodge slightly bigger than all the others. 'XT28E,' I whispered. It *had* to be.

This was it! This was Granny Joss's proof! She *had* found the star that was now a planet, and this was the photographic evidence!

It was time to tell the world.

I ran along the landing and burst into Mum and Dad's room. 'I've got the proof!' I yelled.

Dad sat bolt upright in bed. He wore a black eye mask, and in his sleepiness struggled to take it off properly. 'Whassgoinnon?' he mumbled. His hair stuck up in three different directions.

I switched on the bedroom light and shoved the glass plate in Mum and Dad's faces. 'Granny Joss took a photo of the star and only *thinks* she threw it out! Grandad Wilf kept it in his workshop all these years!'

Mum fumbled on the bedside table for her glasses and she and Dad studied the photograph closely. 'That could be anything,' Dad frowned.

We didn't have time for this. 'Just trust me,' I said. I made a mental list of all the things we'd need for our journey. 'It's proof. Let's get packing.'

'Matilda,' Dad said in a warning tone. 'Stop.'

'What? We've got to go to Stockholm!'

'It's far too early, love,' Mum soothed. 'Why don't we talk more about this in the morning?'

'But—'

'No,' Dad interrupted, his voice extraceedingly quiet and steady. 'Your granny is not trekking halfway round the world to Sweden based on some old photo of goodness knows what. We're doing things the proper way. End of conversation. Go back to bed.' He pulled his eye mask back over his eyes and lay down again.

'It's not just some old photo of goodness knows what,' I muttered. 'It's proof.'

But Dad just ignored me.

Remember that famous guy I mentioned earlier, Thomas Edison? No one supported him when he was trying to invent the light bulb, because they thought he was a failure. When he finally did invent it, it was his 1000th attempt at doing so. 1000th! Most people would have given up long before their *100th* go, especially if everyone kept telling you you'd never do it.

But then we'd all still be sitting in the dark, wouldn't we?

When someone asked him, 'How did it feel to fail a thousand times?' Thomas Edison replied, 'I didn't fail a thousand times. The light bulb was an invention with a thousand steps.' Thomas Edison is a bit of a hero of mine. You might have guessed.

So I knew better than to argue. I knew better than to say, 'Actually, Dad, Sweden is only eleven hundred miles away. I looked it up on the internet just now, so not *really* halfway round the world, but I do know what you're getting at.'

And I knew better than to give up at the first attempt.

7

THE LADIES' BRIDGE

I didn't go back to bed.

I crept around my room, throwing whatever I'd need for an exciting adventure into my rucksack: sketch-book and pencil, bag of jelly babies, a bottle of water, screwdriver, spanner and a pair of pliers, tape measure, Granny Joss's photographic plate (I was extraceedingly careful with that and wrapped it up in an old jumper for safety) and, of course, The Handy-Handy-Hand.

From under my bed, I took out the Tupperware box of money I'd stashed there. I'd been saving for a little while now, ever since The Handy-Handy-Hand had been granted a UK patent, because I wanted to go international.

I'd learned a little trick from Dame Ellen MacArthur, see. In 2005, she broke the world record for the fastest time to sail round the globe on her own. Can you imagine it? Alone at sea, with waves as high as two double-decker buses crashing down around you, the nearest people the ones manning the International Space Station above you. When she was my age, Ellen wanted to buy her first boat but wasn't given any pocket money, so she saved her lunch money instead. She bought only baked beans and mashed potatoes from the school canteen because they were the cheapest items on the menu and put the rest of the money towards her goal. She did that *every single day* for *eight whole years*. Baked beans and mashed potatoes every single day for eight years! What a gal! I've watched all her TED talks, you know.

So I eat vegetarian pasta bake for lunch every day because it only costs £1.30 and I can save the remaining £1.70 of what Dad gives me towards my international patent, which costs a few thousand pounds. I've been doing that for six months now and if I never see another vegetarian pasta bake again, it'll be too soon, but I have to do it if I want to reach my goal. I know the other kids think I'm weird. Let's see how weird they think I am when you can buy The Handy-

Handy-Hand at multiple outlets worldwide and I am a total YouTube star, shall we?

That said, my international patent would have to wait a while. Mum and Dad may not think so, but getting Granny Joss – and her photographic plate – to Sweden by Sunday was more urgent. We couldn't sit around and wait a month for the Prime Minister to respond. *This* was the only way.

As the sun was slowly rising, I changed out of my pyjamas into a pair of blue dungarees over my favourite purple T-shirt, the one with a chart of the elements and the words *I wear this T-shirt periodically* on it. Cos it's the periodic table, see? I love it.

I wrapped up warm in my navy duffel coat, slipped on my white Converse and then, checking Mum and Dad were still asleep, snuck down the stairs and out the front door.

I'd never done anything like this – running away from home – in my life. But it was for Granny Joss. I'm *sure* Mum and Dad would be fine about it. Eventually. By the time I left for university, perhaps.

I didn't pass a single soul as I walked to Granny Joss's. It was a Saturday morning, so maybe people were treating themselves to a nice little lie-in. Also, and this might be unrelated, it was 4.53 a.m.

As I rounded the corner to Canterbury Cares Care Home, my heart leaped into my mouth. All the lights were on downstairs and parked in the driveway was a police car. And I knew – I just knew – who it was for.

I burst through the front doors of the home and ran into the lounge. It was packed full with people – every single resident was there, in their pyjamas and nightdresses, pretending to watch the TV, but really listening to a policeman telling somebody off.

That somebody was Granny Joss.

'– waste of valuable police resources, having to locate you and bring you home,' the policeman moaned to her.

There was a real buzz around the common room. Everyone was giddy at being up so early, for no one had ever tried to escape from the care home before. Nobody had really wanted to, for it was a pleasant enough place, and the residents weren't prisoners or anything.

A couple of ladies behind me whispered, 'I heard she was heading to an airfield!'

Two old men in matching purple dressing gowns at the cards table muttered to each other during their game of *Snap!* 'The lady's got some pluck, that's for sure—'

And right in the corner by the bookcases, one old man in a pair of navy boat shoes said to himself: 'Thirteen knots to the west and thar she blows!' But I figured that wasn't really relevant to this particular scenario.

I bounded right up to them. 'What's going on?' I cried, ignoring the policeman frowning down on me.

'Matilda, love,' Granny Joss said, surprised, 'what are you doing here?'

It was only then that I realized Granny Joss was clutching her handbag and wearing her red winter coat, knitted white jumper, thick woolly brown trousers and hiking boots. A thought whizz-popped into my brain. 'I'm doing the same thing as you!' I cried. 'Heading for Sweden!'

Granny Joss looked sheepish, but before she could say anything, a lady in a blue pinny came over to us. I recognized her as the care home manager, Miss Haggard. She was nice enough, but constantly frazzled and stressed. 'I've notified Mrs Moore's son,' Miss Haggard said to the policeman. 'He wasn't very pleased to be woken up at this hour, but he'll be here shortly.'

I looked at Granny Joss and gulped. It wouldn't be long before my parents realized I wasn't tucked up in bed. We were both going to be in so much trouble. And not only because it was the *second* time that morning Dad had been woken unexpectedly.

'Very well,' the policeman nodded. 'I'll leave you to it. But Mrs Moore,' he added, 'don't make a habit of running away.' He shot one last stern look at both of us, and then allowed Miss Haggard to escort him from the room.

I couldn't help but feel guilty McGuilty. Breaking out of the care home had been my idea after all. 'I'm sorry—' I started.

Granny Joss held up her hand to stop me. 'No!' she said firmly. 'It was *my* moment of madness, not yours. You're not to blame.'

'I need to show you something,' I said shyly, reaching into my rucksack. I realized she'd *just* got into trouble with a policeman, but I couldn't *not* show her the glass plate. 'I found this!'

Granny Joss gasped in surprise. 'How did you—?' she stuttered. 'Where did you—?' A smile spread across her face as she clasped the plate in her hands and peered at it curiously. 'I haven't seen this in years,' she murmured. Her eyes welled with tears. 'Do you know, I took this the very night I discovered XT28E.'

As Granny Joss wiped her face, an elderly lady who had been sitting quietly by the window shuffled over to us. 'Hello,' she beamed. 'I'm Gladys, and I've never told anyone this before, but I'm responsible for Waterloo Bridge in London.'

The effects of zero sleep and creeping out of my house so early were starting to kick in. My eyelids felt heavy. 'What's that now?' I asked.

'In 1941,' Gladys continued, 'we were in the middle of the war, so it was up to the women to do the men's jobs. They were off fighting, but Waterloo Bridge needed rebuilding. There was something wrong with the original's foundations and it had been badly damaged during the Blitz. So *we* did it. Young women of all backgrounds came together, rebuilt it, and several months later, *voilà*! The bridge was completed.'

'That's fantastic!' I said. Building bridges? Girls doing kick-ass work? This was *my* kind of story. 'I bet everyone was *so* grateful!'

'That's just it, child,' Gladys said. 'We didn't get *any* thanks. When the war was over, there was an official ceremony to open the bridge. One politician said—' Gladys closed her eyes, reciting the words exactly as she'd heard them over seventy years ago – 'that "The men who rebuilt Waterloo Bridge are fortunate men. They know that although their names may be forgotten, their work will be of pride and use to London for many generations to come."' Gladys opened her eyes. 'See,' she whispered, 'our *names* weren't all that was forgotten – so was our *very contribution*.'

I looked hard at her. I thought I could see where this was going.

'We've all heard about Sweden,' Gladys continued. The other residents murmured in agreement. 'And we absolutely think you should go,' she said.

My nerves crackled with energy at that. All thoughts of fatigue drifted away. 'What?'

Gladys looked down at her slippered feet, the blue veins running up her calves. 'My legs barely take me up the stairs these days,' she said. 'But if I had the strength to get to The Ladies' Bridge — Waterloo Bridge — and put things right, well, believe you me, I'd be out of here like a shot.'

'Amen to that!' an elderly chap with a twirly white moustache cried from the other side of the lounge.

Gladys took both my and Granny Joss's hands in hers and squeezed them tightly. 'So you must,' she insisted. 'You and I have been overlooked for too long, Joss. Firstly because we're women and now because we're somewhat long in the tooth. So you must go. For all of us!' I opened my mouth to say something, but Gladys tightened her grip. 'For justice!' she cried.

'For justice!' everyone chorused around the lounge.

'And glory!' the twirly-moustached man boomed.

'And seagulls!' the old man in the boat shoes cried, but again, I wasn't entirely convinced he was part of the same conversation.

Granny Joss and I locked eyes. We could each tell what the other was thinking:

– *Is she for real?*

– *Should we?*

— Could we?

— It is the right thing to do, isn't it?

— Is there any cake left from last night?

That last one just popped into my head. I hadn't eaten any breakfast.

'Go! Now!' Gladys urged. 'Before your family arrive. We'll help.'

I looked at Granny Joss, still clutching the glass plate. 'I mean, we *have* got proof now,' I smiled.

Granny Joss looked from me to the plate to Gladys. 'Really?' she whispered. 'You'd really help us?'

Every single care home resident scraped back their chair and struggled to their feet. 'Try and stop us,' the twirly-moustached man cried. He offered a salute, and the rest of the residents copied him in delight.

'It would be our very great pleasure,' Gladys grinned.

8

THE ESCAPE FROM THE
CARE HOME BIT

'Quickly!' one of the residents hissed, looking out the window. 'Your son is here, Joss!'

Outside, the sound of a car door slamming. Footsteps crunched on gravel. 'Mr Moore,' Miss Haggard called from the front steps. 'Please come into my office. I've sent Liz to fetch your mother.'

Inside the lounge, the man with the twirly moustache saluted again. 'Deploy the marbles!' he cried.

The two men at the cards table reached into their pockets and each pulled out a bag of glass marbles. With mischievous grins, they scattered the marbles all over the floor. Everyone watched as they rolled across the carpet, lying in wait.

At that moment, a wiry care home assistant with a head of frizzy black curls burst into the lounge. 'I'm looking for Joss Moooooooore—' Liz's words turned into a yelp as she slipped on the marbles beneath her feet. She frantically floundered around, arms out for balance, but her legs gave way and she fell flat on her back with a loud, 'Oof!'

Gladys turned to Granny Joss and me. 'NOW!' she hissed.

We had no time to lose. 'This way!' I cried. We carefully picked our way across the lounge, avoiding the marbles beneath us, before stepping over Liz's flailing body as she struggled to get back up.

Granny Joss and I raced out of the lounge and along the corridor to the patio doors at the back of the home. Just as the exit was within reach, we heard a voice coming from the room to our right.

'– Don't know what this hullaballoo's about,' it huffed. 'There's too much work to be done, let alone running around like lunatics—'

I peeked my head round the door. Inside the room, the cleaner, a small lady with blue hair, was on her hands and knees, scrubbing away at the skirting boards. She was right inside the doorway – there was no way we could run past without being caught.

Blast! We *couldn't* have had help to escape yet not even get as far as *leaving* the care home!

An idea popped into my head. A little further back down the corridor stood the cleaners' laundry basket. Unlike the wicker basket in my bedroom (that, according to Mum, I never put any of my dirty clothes in, instead leaving them strewn all over the floor or the bannisters or my bed), this was an industrial-sized laundry basket, big enough to hold all the tablecloths and napkins of the care home. It was as big as the wheelie bins outside my school.

'Granny Joss,' I whispered, pacing back along the corridor. I could hear the commotion the marbles had caused still raging on inside the lounge. 'Get in!'

Granny Joss looked from me to the huge laundry basket and back again, unconvinced.

'I've got a plan,' I said reassuringly, even though that plan was basically, *Get in the basket*. 'I'll push.' I opened my rucksack. 'Do you want to put your handbag in here? Just in case?' Granny Joss didn't even ask 'Just in case what?' but plonked her bag inside. I took the photographic glass plate from her and carefully placed that inside too, lifted my rucksack

65

back on my shoulders and clasped my hands together in front of me. 'I'll give you a leg up,' I said. I'd *never* seen her look so surprised. But, to her total credit, Granny Joss placed her left foot inside my clasped hands. What a trouper!

I heaved upwards with all my might. Granny Joss grabbed hold of the top of the laundry basket and, with a giantanic amount of effort, thrust herself inside. 'Waaaaaahhh!' she cried as she toppled onto a heap of pillowcases and towels.

I gripped onto the edge of the basket. It was too high for me to peer inside, even on tiptoe. 'Granny!' I whispered. 'Are you all right?'

Granny Joss emerged at the top of the basket, a napkin stuck to her head. I had to stifle the urge to laugh at the sight of it entangled in her frizzy white hair. 'Let's just get out of here,' she huffed.

I peered under the laundry basket and, spotting a lever at the bottom – the brakes – kicked at it. 'Sorry it's not a Meals on Wheels trolley,' I giggled, wheeling the basket along the corridor to the patio doors. I struggle sometimes with the shopping trolley when we're in Tesco, trying not to bump into the displays of tinned tomatoes. This was even heavier, with a much more precious cargo inside. I whistled a little tune, as if a twelve-year-old wheeling an industrial-sized laundry basket in a care home was the most normal thing in the world. We were almost there!

'What do you think you're doing?' a voice said in my ear.

I nearly jumped out of my skin. I turned to see the cleaner behind me, arms folded, looking at me with very obvious suspicion.

'I-I said to Miss Haggard I'd help,' I stuttered. 'There was such a big' – I tried to remember the word the cleaner had used a moment ago – '*hullaballoo* going on in there.' I jerked my head back towards the lounge. 'As if you haven't got enough to do.'

The cleaner wiped her hands on her pinny, taking me in. 'Thank you,' she said after a moment, breaking into a smile. 'It's about time they knew how overworked I am. Park it by the back door, there's a love.'

I dabbed my coat sleeve along my brow to mop up the beads of sweat that had recently gathered there, then continued towards the patio doors.

'Well done, Matilda,' Granny Joss called from inside the basket. Her voice was muffled, buried as she was under the mound of cloth, but I appreciated the encouragement, nonetheless.

'What was that?' the cleaner asked, suddenly reappearing at my shoulder. Honestly, she was like a bat, with her hearing.

'Oh, nothing. Nothing,' I stuttered. 'Uh, iced bun,' I said. 'Iced bun, Matilda. I really fancy one. Ha ha ha. Byeeeee.' In one swift move, I opened the patio doors and wheeled the basket straight through.

I made a big show of parking the basket against the back wall, like she'd asked me to. I whistled my little 'nothing to see here' tune again and tightened my rucksack straps, all the while aware that the cleaner was watching my every move.

The din from the lounge had died down. I could no longer hear Gladys or the other residents. Any moment, Dad would come looking for me and Granny Joss. We had to leave – NOW!

'Come on,' I hissed under my breath, willing the stupid cleaner to return to her work and stop watching me like a hawk. 'Go away!'

After what felt like an eternity, the cleaner picked up a duster from her bucket and wandered off to carry on with her duties. At last!

'Granny Joss?' I whispered, turning back to the laundry basket.

Except it wasn't there.

The industrial-sized laundry basket was currently flying down the garden path.

'GRANNY JOSS?!' I hissed. I must have forgotten to put the brakes on! Oh, please don't let me have killed her!

From inside the basket came a muffled 'Ai-Ai-Ai-Ai-Ai' as Granny Joss lurched up and down. The basket shot through the back gate of the care home and sailed clean over the pavement, where it landed, very neatly and without too much of a bump, smack bang in the middle of the road.

Smack bang in the middle of the *main* road, right into the path of an oncoming vehicle.

9

THE FASTEST MILK FLOAT IN THE WEST CANTERBURY REGION

1128 miles to Stockholm

Luckily for everyone involved, the oncoming vehicle in question was a milk float, currently travelling slower than a sloth pretending to be a snail.

The laundry basket had careered down the garden path just as an elderly milkman called Joe Squires was finishing up his morning round. He'd had a productive Saturday, delivering pints of full-fat, semi-skimmed, skimmed milk and orange juice to 137 residents of Arnos Yarm so far, and a carton of almond milk to lactose-intolerant Mrs Grantham at 47 Cherry Tree Lane.

But nothing had prepared him for the sight of an elderly lady toppling out of a laundry basket into the middle of the road, right in front of him.

Joe Squires braked suddenly, the milk float screeching to a halt. 'Oh, my days!' he exclaimed, wiping his glasses to check what he was seeing.

'Well, don't just stand there,' Granny Joss called, sprawled on the ground. 'Can you help me up?'

Joe Squires climbed down from behind the wheel as I tore along the garden path of the care home. 'Granny Joss,' I cried, 'are you OK?'

Between us, a confused Joe Squires and I helped Granny Joss to her feet. 'You're lucky I was slowing down,' Joe said. 'I could have driven right into you.'

I felt so guilty McGuilty at that. Killing Granny Joss at the first hurdle wasn't part of the plan. Not that we *had* a plan. And not that killing Granny Joss at *any* hurdle was part of *any* plan, either.

It was clear we were going to need help.

'That's all right, sir,' I said, an idea whizz-popping into my brain. 'We won't sue.'

Joe Squires's eyebrows shot up.

'. . . Iffffffffff you just drop us off at Dover,' I finished.

With that, I guided Granny Joss to the back of the milk float and, for the second time that morning, clasped my hands together. Granny Joss knew what to do by now and so, with another huge heave, I boosted her into the back of the vehicle. She managed to sit herself down on an upturned crate and gripped onto the side of the float. 'It's a bit of a squeeze,' she called.

'Wait! You can't do this. It's a Saturday,' Joe Squires protested. 'It's my busiest day.'

I placed my hands on the sides of the float and heaved myself into the back of it. I squished in next to Granny Joss. 'Ready when you are,' I called. 'We don't have all day!' If we had *any* hope of getting to Stockholm City Hall, we had to get going.

Joe Squires couldn't believe what was happening. Had he *really* been railroaded, by an elderly lady with Einstein-crazy white hair and a young girl with an unnerving spirit, into driving all the way to Dover?

(You may be wondering how I know this. Let's just say that people were *extraceedingly* keen to tell me their version of events after everything had happened. They wanted the world to know just what parts they'd played. So, go with it when I tell you about their journeys, OK?)

Because at that precise moment in time, when I was balancing in the back of the milk float bound for Dover, I had no idea AT ALL of the adventure we'd be going on, or the people we would meet. At that precise moment in time, in the back of a milk float driven by a doddery old man, I was extraceedingly doubtful we'd even make it to the end of the street, to be honest.

10

HIP HIP HOORAY! HIP HIP HOORAY! HIP HIP— OOH, ME HIP!

Back at the care home, the commotion had calmed to the point where everything was bordering on 'normal' once more. The glass marbles had been tidied away. The cleaner had *no idea* that the laundry basket was upturned in the middle of the road. And the man with the twirly moustache had been *very* convincing when he'd told Dad that Granny Joss wanted to be left alone while she sat in the garden and thought about the trouble she'd caused. In a stroke of genius, Gladys had shuffled to the bottom of the lawn, wearing one of Granny Joss's old coats. So as Dad peered out of the lounge window into the garden beyond, he had no reason *not* to think that the figure in the red coat with white hair was his mum. He would let her sit there for a bit, before confronting her about what she'd done.

The rest of the care home was completely deserted, for every remaining resident that had *not* escaped was upstairs on the second floor, crowded round the bay window on the landing, taking turns to look through the telescope.

They watched with glee as Granny Joss and I climbed into the back of the milk float. A resounding 'HOORAY!' echoed throughout the care home as they saw Joe Squires start his engine and drive off, with his precious cargo of me and Granny Joss inside.

Granny Joss was an inspiration to old people everywhere. She hadn't given up at the first attempt. She would be overlooked no longer! If anyone could hotfoot it to Sweden in time to stop Professor Smocks, Joss Moore could.

And maybe, just maybe, this would work out after all.

11

THE WHITE CLIFFS OF DOVER

Arnos Yarm wasn't far from Dover, a mere twenty minutes by car. Or ninety-five excruciatingly slow minutes by milk float; for since Joe Squires had had one rather disturbing road accident that morning, he was *not* about to have another. He kept his speed at a steady 10 mph. Which, when driving on the motorway as the route to Dover took us, wasn't ideal.

I ignored the stares from the queue of irate drivers piled up behind us. They could do nothing but crawl along, tooting their horns in frustration at this old man and his two passengers squished in the back. Instead, I retrieved my sketchbook from my rucksack and my pencil from behind my ear and drew a quick diagram. It was shaky, what with being jostled about all over the shop, but it was my way of saying thanks.

Hey? Guess what? You're going to learn some facts in this book. Some actual facts that you can use to amaze your family next time you're watching *Pointless*. Like:

MATILDA MOORE'S FASCINATING FACTS #1

The port of Dover is the nearest English port to France, at just 21 miles away. Situated in Kent, it is the world's busiest passenger port. Travelling through it each year are:

16 million people

2.1 million lorries

2.8 million cars and motorcycles

86,000 coaches

1 milk float (just once, just this year)

YOU ARE MOST WELCOME, AND THE GLORY OF BEING THE BEST KNOW-IT-ALL SHALL BE YOURS!

As Joe Squires steered the milk float into the car park next to the port, it seemed as if all 16 million travellers were here, for Dover was a-hustling and a-bustling with cars, lorries and coachloads of tourists ready to cross the Channel to France. The vehicles were in four lines, inching towards the large white ferry docked at the end of the port. A man in a yellow jacket and helmet was waving everybody forward.

Joe Squires held up a shaking hand to help me down. I jumped to the ground, before turning to help Granny Joss.

'You're a true gent,' she said to Joe Squires. He still looked completely stunned, in all honesty. 'You've been more helpful than you'll ever know.'

I ripped out the page I'd been working on from my sketchbook and presented it to Joe. 'I've had a few thoughts,' I said, 'about how you can make the suspension of the milk float less bumpy, allowing you a smoother journey and decreasing the rattling of milk bottles.'

Joe Squires looked at me in amazement, like I was Emily Cummins or something. 'That's incredible,' he said.

I shrugged. 'Not really. It's just physics.'

Joe Squires cocked his head to one side and then thrust my bit of paper back at me. 'Sign it for me, please,' he said. 'I reckon you'll be famous one day.'

I quickly jotted my signature on the paper. 'Thanks for the lift,' I said, handing it back to him.

'You're most welcome,' Joe said, and we both watched as he climbed back into his milk float and drove off out of the car park and out of our lives.

'Well, he was nice,' I said. What a spot of luck, being run over by a lovely man who dropped us off where we needed to go. *And* one who thought I was going to be a famous inventor.

'So, what do we do now?' Granny Joss asked.

My stomach growled. I'd forgotten to eat breakfast. From my rucksack, I took out my bag of sweets. 'Well,' I said, biting the head off a green jelly baby, 'we've got enough money to buy tickets for the ferry, but neither of us has a passport. Yours expired, and I've never left the country before.' I looked to the steward in the yellow jacket, waving the cars forward. 'Maybe some family will take pity on us, and let us sit in their boot? We can't just walk on, can we?'

Granny Joss frowned as she chewed her jelly baby. 'I don't think so,' she said in between mouthfuls. 'You know, I was so caught up in the excitement of running away, I didn't really think about *how* we'd get to Sweden.'

I tapped my chin, looking all about me. There had to be something we could do.

To the left of us was the car park leading to the docked ferry. To the right, a little marina, where smaller, privately-owned boats were stationed. Beyond that, I could just about make out a large group of people gathered on the marina dock under the sign 'DOVER'S ANNUAL DIP!' Some were in wetsuits and goggles, ready to launch themselves into the English Channel. Some were clearly there for moral support, holding banners with things like:

YOU CAN DO IT, MUM!

FRED JONES SWIMS FOR CANCER RESEARCH!

And also:

GOLF SALE THIS WAY

But I wasn't quite sure if that was to do with the charity swim or not.

'Maybe *we* could swim?' I said, gazing out across the Channel. I didn't have to look at Granny Joss to know what the answer would be. I'd already risked breaking her hips and the majority of her bones in a wheeled laundry basket that had a mind of its own. Making her swim the Channel might be pushing it.

'Hang on a minute,' I said, a thought whizz-popping into my brain. 'Privately-owned boats! Come on!' I took Granny Joss by the hand and we tore across the car park towards the marina. 'Maybe we can convince someone to take us to France!'

There must have been a dozen boats of various sizes – though none as big as the ferry – inside the marina. *Someone* had to take pity on us. We approached the first boat.

'Hello?' I called, peering onto the deck. 'Anyone there?' There was no sign of movement.

I turned to move onto the next boat, but something shot out between my ankles and I tripped over before I could steady myself. The remaining jelly babies went flying from my hand, scattering all over the dock.

Whatever had leaped out soon leaped on the jelly babies, snaffling them all up in one go. I got back on my feet, dusted myself off and peered at the scraggly, scrawny mess in front of me.

It was a little dog – a terrier. I guessed it had once been light brown, but it was so dirty and its hair so matted that it looked like it slept, bathed and generally hung out 24/7 in mud. 'Poor thing,' Granny Joss muttered beside me.

'Why?' I huffed. 'That poor thing tripped *me* up! And it has eaten our supplies!'

The sorry excuse of a dog had wolfed the remaining jelly babies and looked up at me with sad, haunting, *hungry* eyes. 'Shoo!' I said, waving my hands at it. 'Go away!' We didn't have time for this.

I moved to the next boat docked in the marina, a rusty old thing with pieces of wood missing from the hull. There was no one on that boat either. 'For goodness' sake!' I yelled in frustration. 'Doesn't anyone who owns a boat ever sail it?'

Turns out, actually, no. Granny Joss and I tried a further nine boats and not one single owner was on board. This was ridiculous!

Just then, I sensed someone beside us. I looked down to see the scraggly dog trotting alongside. 'I haven't got any more food,' I yelled, exasperated. 'THERE'S. NO. MORE. FOOD!'

But the dog was rubbish at understanding English, because it padded on beside us, with little regard for my lack of patience or lack of tasty food products. It had found a friend. I was still trying to shoo the dog away when I heard a voice behind us call, 'Can I help you?'

A man in a yellow jacket with 'BORDER PATROL' emblazoned on it approached us. 'Are you lost?'

'Um,' I replied, my brain whirring for an excuse. 'No, we're looking for a friend of ours.'

'And they own one of these boats, do they?' the man asked, gesturing up and down the marina.

'Uh-huh,' I lied, nodding enthusiastically. Somewhere behind me, the little dog barked. That was all we needed.

'Right,' the man replied. 'It's just that we've had reports of a girl and a lady peering in all of the boats along here. That wouldn't be you, would it? Acting suspiciously?'

'Um,' I said again, 'well, yes, but that's only because we've forgotten which one is his.'

'Hmm,' the border patrol guard mused, his eyes scanning my face. I could tell he didn't believe me. 'Fine. I'll level with you. I've been working twenty-four hours straight. It's cold. It looks like rain. We've got the police on our backs all the time, what with the latest refugee crisis. Plus, there's a charity swim across the Channel this afternoon, so we're doubly busy. But we can't be letting people wander aimlessly around the marina. Do you understand?'

Granny Joss and I nodded in unison.

'So do you know someone on these boats or not?' he asked wearily. 'And can someone please tell that flaming dog to stop yapping?'

I glanced over my shoulder. The little dog paced up and down beside a small white boat, the last one docked in the marina – the only one we *hadn't* tried – its scraggly little tail flicking back and forth. I could just about make out two figures pottering around on deck. The dog barked at us, as if calling us to join it.

It was our only hope.

'Ah,' I said, pointing at the boat, 'there he is. That's my . . . uncle. Thanks, anyway.' I grabbed Granny Joss's hand and we calmly walked away from the border patrol guard towards the last boat in the marina. 'Is he still looking?' I hissed.

Granny Joss glanced behind her. 'Yes,' she replied glumly. 'Act normal.' Normal? There was *nothing* normal about any of this.

As we approached the boat, the figures on board came into view. A man in his fifties, with sun-kissed skin and salt-and-pepper hair, heaved his mooring rope from the dock. He wore a navy blue blazer, beige-coloured trousers and a white sailing cap perched jauntily on his head. 'Shut up!' the man yelled at the dog, still yapping on the dock.

MATILDA MOORE'S FASCINATING FACTS #2

A dog's sense of smell is 1000 times more sensitive than a human's.

(No wonder he could smell food a mile off.)

A glamorous blonde lady in a slinky red dress that would have looked more at home on a cruise ship in the Mediterranean than a small boat in Dover placed a hand on the man's shoulder. She carried a plate of freshly-cooked bacon in the other hand. 'Hush, darlink,' she said to the man. She had an accent that I couldn't quite place. Polish, maybe. Or Russian? 'The poor little think is just hungry.' She waved the plate of bacon towards the dog.

It started salivating at that. Jelly babies *and* bacon in the same morning? This was its best day ever! The glamorous lady threw a rasher of bacon onto the dock and laughed as the dog wolfed it down. It looked up hungrily, beady eyes pleading for more.

An idea whizz-popped into my head. This could go the way of Joe Squires if we played it right. 'Hey!' I called as I approached the boat. 'That's my dog!' I couldn't actually bring myself to pat the beast on the head, or to stroke its scraggly, matted fur. They'd just have to take my word for it.

The glamorous lady looked me up and down, her eyes accusatory. 'He was hungry,' she said. 'And when was the last time he had a bath?'

Time to activate *Phase One*.

'Sorry,' I stuttered. 'It's just . . . we've come such a long way. Would you mind if it – he – had a *little* more bacon? He's starving.' If I had learned anything about this animal in the last twenty minutes, it was that he would stop at nothing for food.

The woman raised a perfectly-groomed eyebrow at me, but then held the plate of bacon out to the dog once more. And that was all the invitation he needed.

With an energetic leap, the dog bounded aboard the boat, almost knocking the woman over. As she stumbled on the deck, she barged into her husband, knocking the mooring rope out of his hands. The plate of bacon went flying into the air, landing with a CRASH! on the deck. The dog didn't care, skilfully picking out the bits of bacon on the ground.

I took this opportunity to clamber aboard. I held out my hand and half pulled, half heaved Granny Joss behind me. *Phase One* complete!

I held onto the mast in the centre of the boat and leaned over to wave at the border patrol guard, still watching us from along the dock. 'Nothing to see here!' I called. 'All is completely normal!'

'What do you think you're doing?' The glamorous woman glared at me, holding out her arms to steady herself as the boat lurched to one side.

I pretended to scrabble around after the dog, as if I was fussed about retrieving this pet of mine, instead of using this as a means to climb aboard a boat heading for France, having not a passport or single official document on us.

At that moment, the man, who had by now re-adjusted his captain's hat, and coiled up his mooring rope, gave a yelp and pointed behind us. 'Border patrol!' he hissed to his wife. He dashed to the front of the boat and started clicking buttons and pushing levers.

I was just about to say, 'Oh, don't worry, he's watching *us*,' when Granny Joss placed a hand on my arm to stop me.

'Don't,' she whispered. 'They think he's after *them*.'

The man in the captain's hat frantically turned the wheel, before yelling over his shoulder to the glamorous woman, 'Get the rope! The rope!'

'But I am in heels!' the woman moaned. 'I am not dressed for this!' Still, she tottered to the back of the boat and, with a surprising degree of strength, hauled up the rope with the anchor attached.

The boat lurched forward. The dog was still merrily snaffling at the bacon on the floor, oblivious to anything going on around him.

'Quick!' the glamorous lady shouted. 'He's still watchink!' She folded her arms crossly. 'I *told* you to renew your licence!'

Granny Joss and I exchanged a look. We were stowaways on board a criminal's boat! 'This is jolly exciting, isn't it?' Granny Joss whispered in glee.

The captain frantically spun the wheel, trying to steer past all the other docked boats out of the marina.

'Watch it!' I cried, for I'd spotted something the captain hadn't – the boat was sailing into the open waters of the Channel . . . straight into the path of the ferry that had set sail from the dock. The *giantanic* white ferry, about a hundred times bigger than the rusty old boat we were on.

HOOONNNKKKK!!!

A warning horn blasted from the ferry looming over us. We were metres away from crashing into it.

'HANG ON!' the captain yelled.

The ferry dwarfed us in size. It cut through the water like a knife through butter. It was sure to break the boat into mere splinters, sending me, Granny Joss and that stupid dog into a watery grave. I'd seen *Titanic*. I knew how this ended.

I squeezed Granny Joss's hand tightly. Granny Joss squeezed her eyes shut. This was it, then. The world would never know that Planet Smocks was wrongly named. It would never know how brilliant Granny Joss really was. It would never know The Handy-Handy-Hand in over thirty-two territories across the globe.

At that moment, the captain, with all his strength, swung the wheel all the way to the left. With an almighty lurch, the boat veered past the ferry, just manoeuvring itself out of the way in time.

'Waaahoooo!' the captain called, punching the air in delight at his skill. 'What an excellent bit of steering, even if I do say so myself!'

Granny Joss wiped the sweat from her brow. 'I saw my life flashing before my eyes then,' she said breathlessly.

We shakily got to our feet. My stomach felt as if it was in my ankles. That had been one close call. 'At least we made it,' I laughed to Granny Joss. 'We're on our way to France!' AND we hadn't been crushed by a ferry. Which was nice. 'Nothing can stop us!'

The glamorous woman joined her husband at the wheel and they both stared hard at the two stowaways who had caused them such peril. 'You'd better start talking,' the woman said to us, with not so much as a hint of a smile on her face.

I gulped. How was I going to get us out of *this*?

12

DAD'S NOT FOOLED

Gladys had sat on the bench in the garden of Canterbury Cares Care Home for a good half an hour before Dad thought to go and check on Granny Joss. Who very obviously *wasn't* Granny Joss.

Gladys's teeth chattered against the biting December wind. She rubbed her hands together, trying to keep warm. Maybe she could go back inside – we'd had a good head start. She'd heard a big HOORAY! coming from the landing of the care home about twenty minutes earlier, so our escape plan must have worked after all.

She was just starting to dream of a warm cup of tea when Dad's voice piped up behind her. 'Mum?' he called. 'Why don't you come inside? We can talk about this. Mum!'

Oh, how Gladys wished she had the legs of a fifty-year-old so she could make a dash for it. A hand placed itself on her shoulder. 'Mum?' Dad sounded unconvinced now. This didn't *look* like his mother.

Gladys turned round and beamed at him. 'All right, love? Nippy out, isn't it?'

Dad stared, open-mouthed. 'I'm – I'm sorry, I thought you were . . .' His voice trailed off as he looked frantically around the garden. 'You've not seen my mother, have you? Joss Moore?'

Gladys did her best to look innocent. 'Nope,' she replied. 'No, I don't think so.' Her voice caught in her throat. She was suddenly nervous. 'No, I haven't. I mean, not for ages. A day, maybe. Or a month. I forget. I don't think I've seen her since 1997, actually.'

Dad narrowed his eyes at her. He took in the ill-fitting red coat. Something about this was *very* fishy.

And then the penny dropped.

'I don't believe it!' he yelled, dashing back inside the care home. He raced through the residents' lounge, up the stairs and into Granny Joss's bedroom. It was empty, of course. But her coat had gone – and so had her handbag.

Dad pulled his mobile from the pocket of his grey trousers and punched in the number for home. Mum answered after four rings. 'Where's Matilda?' Dad asked.

'What?' Mum yawned, half asleep.

'Go and check her bedroom.'

Mum let out a sigh. 'Hang on,' she said, putting the phone down. Dad paced around Granny Joss's bedroom as he waited for Mum to spot my *obviously* empty bed. 'She's not here,' Mum said breathlessly into the phone after a moment. 'She's— Where *is* she?'

Dad let out a puff of air. 'She's with Mum. And I think we can jolly well guess where they're heading.' He reached into his pocket for his car keys. 'I'll come and get you and then we'll search the streets,' he said, hurrying down the stairs of the care home.

'Right,' Mum said, attempting to keep her voice calm. 'I'll keep trying Matilda's phone.'

'No need to panic,' Dad said, also trying to keep his voice calm. His twelve-year-old daughter and his eighty-year-old mum had got it into their heads to travel to Sweden, with no money or passports or transportation. 'They won't have got very far.'

Oh, how wrong he was.

13

GRANDMAMA OLGA'S EASY-PEASY-LEMON-AND-ORANGE MARMALADE-AND-LEFTOVER-BITS-OF-OLD-TEA-BAG FRUIT CAKE

MATILDA MOORE'S FASCINATING FACTS #3

A single bolt of lightning contains enough energy to cook 100,000 pieces of toast.

(The glamorous woman's stare was more powerful than that.)

As dark clouds rumbled overhead, the woman glared at me, face as hard as flint. 'You had better talk, little girl,' she hissed.

I waved my hands all around me. 'We're in the middle of the Channel,' I said simply. 'You're not going to chuck us into the sea.'

The woman narrowed her eyes. 'I wouldn't be so sure,' she replied.

I looked at the waves. The boat left a trail of churned, choppy froth in its wake. I gulped. The sea air filled my lungs. And also the smell of something else. Was that – was that burning?

'We don't want any trouble,' Granny Joss piped up. 'We're simply trying to get to Sweden, by way of France.'

'You forced your way onto our boat and we almost crashed into a ferry – what's to stop us going to the police?' the glamorous woman said.

A thought whizz-popped into my head. 'You seemed pretty keen to get away from the border patrol guard,' I replied, folding my arms. 'Why?' I wasn't going to be the only one to answer hard questions.

'Yes, well,' the woman blustered, her face suddenly turning red. 'That's, um, different.'

I was just about to say, 'Different *how*?' when suddenly there was a loud BANG! from the back of the boat.

'Oh, no! No no no no no!' the captain cried. He ran the full length of the deck, almost knocking his wife, Granny Joss and me overboard as he barged past. 'Svetlanka? Man the wheel!'

The glamorous woman – Svetlanka – threw her arms up in despair and tottered to take control of the steering.

I followed the captain, curiosity getting the better of me. Wisps of grey smoke poured from the small black engine fixed to the back of the boat. 'We must have ruptured something manoeuvring so erratically out of the marina,' the captain moaned. He wrung his hands in despair. 'I'm no good with this sort of thing.'

I whipped my rucksack off my back and retrieved my screwdriver, spanner and pliers from it. 'I can take a look,' I said, brandishing my tools and clambering over the back seat to examine the engine.

The captain scoffed. 'I don't think so. We'll have to go back.'

Well, *he* could jog on!

'On day fifteen of her world record attempt for the fastest solo circumnavigation of the globe,' I said, 'Dame Ellen MacArthur's main generator broke down. She had to fix it by torchlight. In the dead of night. In sub-zero temperatures. While the boat was zooming round the Cape of Good Hope at sixty knots an hour. I think I can handle a small engine.'

I prodded the box, noting how hot the engine was, and checked the battery and spark plugs. It wasn't dissimilar to the inner workings of a car, and I'd already tinkered around with one of those when I was eight. Dad didn't know, obviously, and I wasn't going to tell him. He made us all sit on plastic bags on every journey so we didn't scratch the leather on the seats. Can you *imagine* how mad he'd get if he knew I had dismantled the engine? 'One of your water pump impellers is broken,' I said matter-of-factly. 'Easily fixed. Pen.'

The captain looked at me in a mixture of shock and amazement.

'In my bag,' I added.

He gave a little start and then rooted inside my rucksack, pulling out both The Handy-Handy-Hand and a black biro. He passed me the pen and I wedged it inside the engine. It was the same shape and size as the broken component of the water pump and, just as I suspected, the engine immediately started to cool down.

'Ta-da!' I said, standing up and taking The Handy-Handy-Hand and my rucksack from the captain.

'But – how did you—?' he spluttered.

I smiled. Svetlanka peered curiously from me to her husband and back again as she kept the boat moving in a steady direction. 'Would someone please care to explain what's going on?' the captain asked, exasperated.

'I'm an inventor,' I said, gesturing to The Handy-Handy-Hand. 'And I'm saving up to get an international patent for this. But that's not even the half of it. Granny Joss should be a famous scientist. We're off to stop the man who prevented her from being one. He's about to be awarded a Nobel Prize.'

The captain and Svetlanka looked at me as if I was some sort of crazy person. I could practically see their minds whirring in wonder. After a moment, the captain stuck out his hand. 'Duck,' he said.

Granny Joss and I stooped low, covering our heads. 'Why?' I cried. 'What's happening?'

The captain blushed. 'No, no,' he said, forcing a laugh. 'That's my name. Christopher Peter Duck.'

I straightened myself out again. 'Wait,' I said, suppressing the urge to giggle. 'Your name's Chris P Duck? Crispy Duck?' There were people in the world stupider than Thomas Thomas's parents?

'I'd rather you didn't bring that up,' Chris P mumbled. 'This is my wife, Svetlanka.'

Svetlanka rolled her eyes. 'I *hate* his name,' she said passionately. 'I refuse to call myself Svetlanka Duck.'

'Sorry about all that business back there, with the border patrol,' Chris P said. 'It's just – well, technically, we don't have a mooring licence to dock in the Dover marina.'

'Pffffft.' Svetlanka let out a puff of air. 'They don't want to hear about that. Come,' she said to Granny Joss and me, 'sit down.' She motioned to the seats carved into the side of the boat, and as we made ourselves comfy she bent down to a cool box and pulled out all manner of drinks, sweets, biscuits and sandwiches from inside. The dog barked in delight at that. I'd half forgotten he was there.

As Granny Joss relayed to Chris P and Svetlanka all about Professor Smocks and the falsely named planet, Svetlanka produced treat after treat for us to enjoy. 'You poor thinks,' she soothed as Granny Joss concluded our tale. 'You've already travelled such a long way and you've still so far to go. Here. You must eat this.' She produced a curious-looking brown cake, with speckles of orange peppered through it. 'And you too,' she added, dropping a chunk onto the deck for the dog to snaffle.

Granny Joss helped herself to a large slice. 'Mmm,' she said, crumbs spraying everywhere. 'I've never tasted anything like it.'

'It was Grandmama's secret recipe,' explained Svetlanka. 'No one else in the world knows how to make it.' Suddenly tears welled up in her eyes.

'Are you all right?' asked Granny Joss.

Svetlanka sniffed. 'Grandmama Olga died many years ago,' she said, her voice barely a whisper. 'But her recipe was passed down from her to my mother and from my mother to me. Well,'

Svetlanka added, 'it was passed down to me *and* my sister.' She sniffed. 'We were separated, twenty years ago.'

'Oh dear,' Granny Joss murmured.

Svetlanka leaned back against the side of the boat, her long legs entwining each other. 'I come from Kosovo, originally. My parents divorced when I was ten years old, my sister twelve. My mother brought me to England to start a new life, my father took my sister to Europe. Over the years, we lost contact. I've tried to find out what happened to her, but each time I hit a dead end. It's like she doesn't want to be found.' She let out a sob.

'That's awful!' I said. I couldn't even begin to imagine how sad that must have been. I reached out my hand.

Svetlanka took it in hers and squeezed it. 'Thank you,' she whispered.

Which was all rather sweet, but actually *super* awkward – I'd been reaching out to take a slice of cake. I wanted to see what all the fuss was about. 'Uh, may I?' I asked, nodding to the cake. Svetlanka smiled and gave me an extra big slice.

But before I could shove it in my mouth, a voice cried out somewhere in the water beside us, 'HELP!'

We all peered over the side of the boat.

In the sea, a rather large, round-bellied chap was treading water furiously. He wore a pink swimming cap, his goggles askew on top of his head, and he was taking deep breaths, trying not to swallow half the Channel. 'I'm-ever-so-sorry-to-trouble-you,' the man panted. 'I-hate-to-ask-but-as-you-can-see-I'm-pretty-desperate. You-couldn't-help-me-out-could-you?'

For a man so out of breath, I couldn't help thinking he was using an awful lot of words simply to say, 'Give us a lift, mate.'

'Not you as well,' Chris P huffed. He'd only just got over the shock of me, Granny Joss and that pesky dog hoodwinking him into a ride.

'He's turning a bit blue,' I said, for the man was clearly not the finest specimen of health. Granny Joss, Svetlanka and I grabbed the man by his arms and heaved with all our might. It was like Captain Ahab attempting to lift Moby Dick. That was a whale, by the way. And I'm not being mean, but it *did* feel as if we too were attempting to lift a whale.

After three attempts, we eventually hoisted the man up and over the side of the boat. He sprawled out on the deck, looking *very* much like a beached whale might if it accidentally found itself out of the water. 'It's like Piccadilly Circus around here,' Chris P Duck huffed. 'I'm going to start charging.'

I helped prop the man up so he could rest against the seat. Granny Joss found a blanket in one of Svetlanka's bags and wrapped it round the man's shoulders. After a few minutes, the colour returned to his cheeks and he was starting to feel quite himself again. He gave a loud sniff. 'Is that bacon I can smell?'

By now, the dog had hoovered up all the remaining pieces of bacon, sweets and biscuits and was sitting happily, wagging his tail, having such a lovely day out.

'If you're well enough to eat, you're well enough to tell us what the flaming heck you're up to,' Chris P said.

The man held out his hand. 'I'm Mickey,' he said. 'I'm swimming the Channel for charity. I know what you're all thinking,' he added, 'and you're right. I haven't exactly done the training. But it's the thought that counts.'

Granny Joss patted his arm. 'Quite right,' she soothed. 'Well done for trying.'

Mickey puffed out his chest. 'I'm planning on winning, you know. There's a medal for the first person to make it. And a prize.'

I leaned across him and peered over the side of the boat. In the distance, I could make out a number of heads bobbing up and down in the water. They were quite some way away, the boat putting a greater distance between us and them as each minute passed.

'All you've got to do is drop me off a little way before Calais, and it'll be like I've swum the whole thing,' Mickey beamed.

'But that's cheating!' I cried.

Mickey shrugged. 'Everyone does it.'

I gestured to the sea of bobbing heads behind us. 'NO ONE ELSE is doing it! Everyone else is swimming!' I had a good mind to throw him back into the sea. 'The whole reason we're on this trip is for justice,' I said. 'And because certain prizes haven't been fairly given.'

As Mickey huddled under the blanket and Svetlanka set about making everyone a cup of tea from a thermos flask and offering around a plate of custard creams, I launched, once more, into why we were Sweden-bound.

To his credit, Mickey listened with ever-widening eyes as he took it all in: Professor Smocks, the planet, the Nobel Prize ceremony. He almost choked on his biscuit as I explained about Thomas Thomas. It was fair to say *that* was the moment I warmed to him.

'Right, then,' Mickey said after I'd finished, blinking the sun out of his eyes and wiping crumbs from round his mouth. 'I'll just let this lot go down, then I'll get back out there.' He smiled at Granny Joss and me. 'You've inspired me, ladies. But I can't swim on a full stomach.'

Everyone laughed at that. A new, positive atmosphere descended on the boat. Even Chris P Duck's bad mood lifted. Largely to do with the fact that Svetlanka offered him an extra-large helping of cake.

'I haven't even asked,' Mickey said, staring towards the back of the boat. 'What's your dog called?' I followed his gaze to see the beast still wagging his tail, basking in the sunshine, stuffed from bacon and biscuits.

'That's a good point,' Granny Joss said. 'We've not thought of a name.'

'Tag,' I replied, almost instantly. The name just popped into my head. 'Short for Tag-along. It's what he's been doing all day.'

'So, he's *not* your dog?' Chris P asked, eyebrows knitted together. A shadow crossed his face. This animal had led them into all sorts of trouble already!

'Ummm,' I stuttered. 'He is now.' And with that, I scooped the dog into my arms and gave him a kiss on the head.

And then I immediately put him down again, leaned over the side of the boat and tried to get some of the salty sea spray into my mouth to wash the taste of muddy, matted dog hair from my lips. Svetlanka was right. This dog *did* need a bath.

As I got up from the side of the boat, something caught my eye. 'Land!' I cried, pointing straight ahead.

Vast stretches of green appeared on the horizon. If I squinted, I could make out other ships in the port, a huge ferry among them, and tiny dots of people milling in and around the harbour. 'We're nearly there!'

Mickey started stretching his arms and legs. 'Right,' he said, 'I'm going to do this! Would you mind circling back a bit and dropping me off with all the others?'

As Chris P swung the boat around, Svetlanka got out a tub of butter from the cool box. 'It was for the bacon sandwiches,' she said, almost apologetically, and while Granny Joss rubbed butter all over Mickey's arms and legs and big belly, greasing him up to keep him warm in the water, he popped his goggles back on and tightened them up.

'Thanks for the lift,' Mickey said, reaching over and shaking everyone's hand. 'I really hope you make it to Sweden,' he added to Granny Joss and me.

So do I, Mickey, I replied silently in my head. *So do I.*

'Good luck, Mickey!' everyone shouted as we helped him clamber up on the back of the boat. After counting to three, Mickey belly-flopped into the water with an almighty SPLASH! He spluttered and clutched at the air for a moment while he found his stride, and then slowly doggy-paddled his way towards shore.

He was immediately overtaken by every single swimmer in the race.

'Keep going, Mickey!' I yelled. 'It's the taking part that counts!' I had to say that – he had no hope whatsoever of winning the honest way.

The boat sped off, until Mickey was a mere speck bobbing up and down behind us. Granny Joss, Svetlanka, Chris P and me all looked at each other. No one could *quite* believe that had happened. 'Well,' I said after a moment. 'He seemed nice.' What a lovely morning we'd had, making new friends and inspiring a cheater to change his ways.

As we got closer to land – and to a signal – my phone buzzed in my pocket. I took out my mobile to see fourteen missed calls from Mum and Dad. And texts. *Lots* of texts.

DAD: Can't find you in Arnos Yarm. On our way to Dover. Stay safe xx

DAD: Pulling into Dover car park now.
Where are you??

MUM: Stop playing games. Call us.
We're worried about you xx

DAD: Matilda. I'm warning you. Where
are you? x

MUM: Come on, love. We're not cross xx

DAD: I'm cross.

CHELSEA: Have u dun maths hmwrk?
Wots answr 2 Q4?

'We should probably call them, love,' Granny Joss said. 'Let them know we're OK.'

I gulped. Now that we'd made it to France, I didn't want anyone making us go home again. Instead, I quickly tapped a message to my parents.

At Calais. Granny Joss and me fine. We'll
be back soon. Ish. Also, we have a dog
now. x

I knew my parents were going to be L. I. V. I. D. Absolutely blow-the-roof-you-are-in-so-much-trouble-young-lady-and-not-just-about-the-dog, but I'd worry about that when we got back.

'That'll do,' Granny Joss nodded. 'As long as they know we're alive.'

As we pulled up to the port, Svetlanka started putting everything away and made the boat tidy again, while I picked up my rucksack and stuffed The Handy-Handy-Hand inside, being careful not to scratch Granny Joss's photographic plate.

Chris P Duck expertly manoeuvred the boat into the dock of Calais, this time avoiding the ferry's path altogether. He cut the engine and dropped the anchor back into the water, and then turned to Granny Joss and me. 'Will you be all right from here?' he asked, his voice full of concern.

Granny Joss nodded. 'Oh yes. I expect we'll get a train to Stockholm. Don't you worry.'

Chris P looked us over for a moment, and then reached inside his navy blazer. From it, he took out a wad of notes, riffled through them and thrust them at

Granny Joss. 'Oh, no!' she protested. 'We couldn't possibly.'

Chris P held up his hand. 'Nonsense,' he said firmly. 'They're euros. You'll not get far without them.' He beamed at me. 'Consider it payment for repairing the engine. I'm sorry I didn't think you could fix it. You did an excellent job.'

I reached over and gave him a giant hug. He was a little taken aback by my gratitude, in all honesty, but he patted me on the shoulder pleasantly in return.

Svetlanka pressed a huge hunk of cake wrapped in clingfilm into my hand. 'Please,' she insisted. 'For the journey.'

I shoved the cake into my duffel-coat pocket, before leaping off the boat to the dock, and turning to help Granny Joss. Tag jumped down to join us. It felt good to be on solid ground once again. 'Thank you,' I said gratefully. 'For everything.'

Chris P and Svetlanka Duck waved as we walked away from the dock, in among the hustle and bustle of Calais, Tag trotting alongside us. I was grateful for his company. Even though I'd only known him for a few hours, Tag was a comforting reminder of England, of home; a friend. And with Granny Joss and I all alone in a strange country, with no real idea of where we were going, a friend at this moment in time was pretty A-OK, actually.

14

OÙ EST LA GARE?

1071 miles to Stockholm

Granny Joss and I, with Tag alongside, wandered through the packed port of Calais. They had border control here too, though they seemed more concerned with keeping crowds of people at bay and not allowing them access to the lorries that were queuing for the ferry back to England than with us. We could just about pass as regular tourists. And no one had even *asked* for our passports!

As we strode out of the main ferry concourse alongside the motorway, with cars, vans and coaches all trundling past, Granny Joss pointed ahead of us. 'That'll do!' she cried, gesturing to a taxi rank at the far end of the port. I gripped hold of Granny Joss's hand as we walked towards the car. Getting separated from each other would be game over, quite frankly.

Granny Joss waved to the only taxi driver in the rank, a hunched-shouldered grumpy old man with a weather-beaten face. He shuffled out of the car and opened the back door for us. '*Où?*' he asked.

In French.

We'd forgotten about that.

'Uh—' I stuttered. I'd only been learning French for a term at Arnos Yarm Comprehensive. So far, we'd mastered how to say our names, how old we were, and that we lived in a small town outside of London.

'*Je m'appelle Matilda,*' I said. '*J'ai douze ans. J'habite dans un petit village près de Londres.*'

The taxi driver looked at me curiously. A thought whizz-popped into my head. I grabbed the euros that Chris P Duck had given us and held them out to the driver. He beamed. *That* did the trick. It seemed that money talked in *whatever* language you used.

Granny Joss and I slid into the back seat of the taxi. I slung my rucksack down in the footwell by my Converse trainers, and Tag leaped onto my lap.

I pumped my arms by my side and made a 'choo-choo' sound. 'Train?' I said in the loud and slow voice that English people use on foreign holidays to make themselves understood by locals. 'Train?' I racked my brains, desperately searching for the French word for it.

Granny Joss was similarly lost in thought. She didn't have a clue about the French language either, but she'd picked up the odd word here and there in her eighty years. 'Mare?' she said, the flicker of a memory coming back to her. '*Sur mer?*'

The taxi driver's eyes lit up. 'Criel-sur-Mer?' he asked, looking between Granny Joss and me, still making the motion of a train.

'That sounds about right,' Granny Joss said, beaming.

'*Si! Si!*' I confirmed, pleased that I'd remembered the word for 'yes'. Unfortunately, I'd remembered the word for 'yes' in Spanish, which was pretty remarkable in itself, seeing as I'd never had a Spanish lesson in my life. But everyone was smiling and looked like they knew what they were doing, so I thrust the euros at the driver and he started the engine.

'*Chien?*' he asked, looking down at Tag in a dubious manner.

117

'Oh yes,' I said. 'He's with us.'

The taxi driver coughed and held out his hand again. It was obvious he wanted more money if he was going to have to cart the dog around too. What a meanington!

I opened the Tupperware box from my rucksack and held out the change to him. He grinned as he rifled through the box, selecting most of the coins in there. There were hardly any left! But there were no other taxis in sight; what choice did we have?

The taxi driver pocketed the coins and sped off down the road, his little Christmas tree air freshener swinging from the rear-view mirror.

I may have been annoyed about the money, but we'd made it to France. We hadn't had to use our passports either. Good thing too – neither of us had one. We were heading to the station to catch the train to Sweden. We were one step closer to our goal. We were one step closer to Stockholm.

And we were one step closer to wiping the smile off Professor Smocks's smug old face.

15

UM, WHERE ARE WE?

I stared out of the window, watching the world go by. My stomach was a mixture of nerves, excitement and custard cream biscuits. Granny Joss, eyes closed, was lightly sleeping beside me. Good. We had quite the journey ahead of us – she needed as much rest as possible.

It was only after a little while that I realized we were getting deeper into the countryside – away from buildings and motorways and traffic. My knowledge of France wasn't brilliant, but I was pretty confident that a train station large enough to house trains heading in all directions – including Sweden – probably wouldn't be surrounded by so much . . . *grass*. Wouldn't it be near the port of Calais for anyone wanting onward journeys?

As if to answer my question, the taxi driver slowed to a halt and pulled over to the side of the road. '*Ici*,' he said, gesturing all around him.

'This is the train station?' I asked, gently shaking Granny Joss awake. She wiped her eyes and slowly took in her surroundings. 'Are we here?' she asked sleepily.

The driver pointed to something in the distance. '*Ici*,' he said again, waggling his eyebrows at us.

Inwardly, I cursed Mademoiselle Dupont. Why wasn't *this* the sort of thing we learned about in French? What a taxi driver waggling his eyebrows means is much more useful than telling someone you go to the cinema once a week and that you don't have any brothers or sisters.

In somewhat of a daze, I grabbed my rucksack, and Granny Joss, Tag and I jumped out of the taxi. The driver screeched the car into a three-point turn and shot off back the way we'd come.

'Well, he was helpful,' I huffed. I looked at Granny Joss. She *did* seem rather tired. Getting just this far was taking its toll. 'Are you OK?' I asked, suddenly concerned. Was Dad right – that this was too much for her?

Granny Joss inhaled a deep breath of French countryside air. As she exhaled, a wave of contentment washed over her face. 'I've never felt better,' she replied.

Good enough for me.

But where to now? I wasn't allowed a fancy mobile, where I could run up an expensive bill searching for Stephanie Kwolek or Phillips Drill Bits on the internet, so I couldn't look on my phone for a map to find out where we were.

Instead, Granny Joss and I walked in the direction the taxi driver had pointed, Tag snuffling the ground for food behind us. Maybe the train station was tucked away out of sight? Maybe its overhead power lines were made of the latest stealth technology, so no one could actually see them? Maybe?

As we walked, a sign in the distance became visible. This must have been what the driver was pointing to. I squinted to see what was written on it. 'Criel-sur-Mer,' I said aloud. 'Population two hundred and six.'

Granny Joss tapped her forehead, suddenly remembering something. '*La gare!*' she cried. 'That's the word! *Où est la gare?*'

My heart sank. I had a funny feeling I knew where this was going. 'Sorry?'

'*La gare* means station,' Granny Joss confirmed, 'not *sur mer*.'

I put two and two together. 'The taxi driver thought we were asking him to take us to Criel-sur-Mer? Instead of "*Où est la gare?*" for the train?'

'Exactly,' Granny Joss said.

Great. We were in *completely* the wrong place. We were lost. Horrendously, terrifically, tragically so.

Now what were we going to do?

16

LIGHTS, CAMERA, ACTION!

1176 miles to Stockholm

MATILDA MOORE'S FASCINATING FACTS #4

If you drilled a tunnel straight through the Earth and jumped in, it would take you exactly 42 minutes and 12 seconds to get to the other side.

(We could have done with that tunnel about now.)

On the internet last night, I'd researched a route to Sweden. From Calais in France, on to Brussels, then Dusseldorf in Germany, crossing the

North Sea at Puttgarden to get to Denmark, then on to Copenhagen and just before we got to Stockholm, Jönköping, Linköping and Norrköping. Yes, I realize that's a lot of köping. And no, at this moment, I wasn't.

That route was 1071 miles from Calais and was *not* based on us sitting on a kerb in Criel-sur-Mer. I had no idea where Criel-sur-Mer was. Apart from 'The Middle Of Nowhere'. And 'Of Absolutely No Use To Us Whatsoever'.

I checked my watch. It was 3.03 p.m. That couldn't be right – the sky was beginning to change from a bruised purple to a dusky charcoal. But it was far too early, even in December.

'They're an hour ahead,' Granny Joss piped up beside me, reading my mind. 'It's just gone four o'clock here.'

I counted on my fingers. The Nobel Prize ceremony was at midday the next day. That gave us twenty hours to get from Criel-sur-Mer to Sweden, without any money, cos the taxi ride had wiped out most of my savings and Chris P Duck's euros.

The task ahead may have seemed impossible, but we couldn't give up. I leaped to my feet. The road stretched out in front and behind us as far as I could

see, but on the other side of the street were woods —
maybe an answer lay through there. 'Fancy exploring?'
I asked Granny Joss.

She shrugged. 'It's the only plan we've got.'

I helped her to her feet and the two of us crossed
the road. 'Tag!' I called, waving to the dog. He had his
face buried in the wild flowers by the side of the kerb,
obviously hoping to find something to eat. 'This way!'

He bounded over and we all traipsed into the woods,
twigs crackling beneath our feet (and paws). 'Good job
you're wearing your hiking boots,' I said to Granny Joss.

The tips of her ears turned pink. 'I knew they'd
come in handy,' she replied, pleased as you like.

After a moment, I heard the sound of a low hum.
It was the sound of a running engine. Yessss! I *knew*
we'd be all right. All we'd have to do was convince the
owner of the vehicle to take us to the train station.
And this time, we knew the word for 'station'.
Nothing could go wrong!

We scrambled through the bracken, the noise
growing louder by the second. It wasn't just one
engine either, but several, alongside cries and shouts.
People! We would have our pick of transportation!

The bracken led to a steep grassy bank. I clasped Granny Joss under the elbow and, together, we slowly climbed up it. When we reached the top, my jaw dropped open. Below us was a field lit by big, heavy floodlights. The whole place was a hive of activity.

At least a hundred people were buzzing about. Some were pushing heavy boxes and machinery, while others gathered round a monitor, watching something on the screen. 'Oh, my,' Granny Joss panted, trying to get her breath back. 'A film set!'

Tag yapped at something across the field – a red food truck, offering hot dogs and burgers to a queue of people – and then a blur of scraggy fur whizzed past me as he scampered down the bank, his tongue lolling out of the side of his mouth as he caught the whiff of sausages. My stomach rumbled as Granny Joss and I carefully negotiated our way down the slope to follow him. The smell of fried onions travelled up my nose. It seemed an awfully long time since we had been eating cake on Chris P's boat.

Tag pawed the side of the food truck, his claws scratching the wheels. 'Excuse me,' I said, as we approached the burly man in a white apron, flipping burgers. I hoped this would go the way of nice, food-providing Svetlanka. 'Could we possibly—?' I gestured to the bread rolls stacked up at the back of the food truck. 'We don't have any money left, but we've come a long way . . .'

The man frowned at Tag, shook his head and continued to serve the people in the queue. Either he didn't understand English or was flat-out refusing to give us any food. What a meanington!

A hand tapped me gently on the shoulder. A pink-haired lady in the queue shyly held out a bag of crisps. 'You can have these,' she said in perfect English. 'I brought them with me in case lunch wasn't included. I think your dog wants some.'

I ripped the bag open gratefully. 'Thank you,' I spluttered in between mouthfuls. I threw a couple of crisps in Tag's direction, and laughed as he wolfed them down. 'What is all this?'

The girl's face turned a brilliant shade of red. Even in the fading light, I could see she was blushing. 'It's Philippe de Bouvier's latest film!' she squealed. 'I'm an extra. Isn't it exciting?'

Granny Joss fished inside the bag of crisps for a handful. 'Who's Philippe de Bouvier?' she asked.

A loud GASP! rang out among the queue of people at the food truck. Everyone turned to glare at Granny Joss. 'Who's Philippe de Bouvier?' they cried. '*WHO'S* Philippe de Bouvier?'

The pink-haired lady looked at us in what I could only describe as pity. 'He's the most famous movie star in France!' she declared, excited and incredulous at the same time.

I looked all around the film set. 'Well, where is he, then?'

The girl traced the ground with her toe. 'We've not seen him yet. He mostly hangs out in his trailer. He's super-famous and super-busy.'

'And anyway,' a tall man behind her butted in, 'he never gives interviews. He's too cool for that. He doesn't talk to *anyone*.'

'I've heard it's because he's really shy,' a middle-aged woman behind him piped up.

This was all very well and good, but we were meant to be on our way to Sweden. 'Is there a train station near here? Or a taxi firm?'

The pink-haired lady shrugged. 'I don't know. We were sent here on a bus. It's not coming back for us till midnight.'

There was no way we could wait that long. Granny Joss squinted in the distance. 'Look!' She pointed to the far end of the field.

'A hot-air balloon?' I cried. I hadn't even spotted it until that moment; my mind was so focused on the food truck and well, *food*, mainly. The balloon had a red and blue striped canopy, with a wooden basket attached underneath.

'Maybe we could ask the pilot to take us to Sweden?' Granny Joss shrugged.

It *had* to be worth a shot! I didn't want Tag scampering off again on the lookout for food, so I shoved him inside my rucksack, being careful not to scratch him with The Handy-Handy-Hand, or for him to scratch Granny Joss's photographic plate. 'Maybe we can hijack it?' I said, totally serious.

Granny Joss frowned as we walked towards the hot-air balloon. 'That's what you wanted to do with a boat in Dover,' she said, equally serious. 'Let's stop trying to hijack things, shall we?'

'Hello?' I called as we reached the hot-air balloon. There was no one near it. 'Hel-oh-oh?' I peered over the top of the wooden basket and almost gave myself a heart attack.

Sitting on the floor of the basket was a muscular man, early twenties maybe, with slicked-back brown hair and dark brooding eyes. His jaw was perfectly square, with a dimple in the middle of his chin. He was dressed all in black, with a pair of old-fashioned flying goggles on his head. The man was chewing his nails nervously, and seemed to be muttering to himself.

Seeing the pilot in the basket, I soon recovered from being startled. 'Hello,' I said, in my best, sweetest voice, 'we need to ask a favour.'

The man looked up at me, eyes wide in confusion. He shook his head – 'I, uh, *non, non comprende.*'

I tapped my head. 'Of course!' I cried. 'You're French. I'm sorry, we don't speak much. What's the word we want, Granny?'

'*Où est la gare?*' Granny Joss said slowly.

I started pumping my arms like a train. 'Choo! Choo!' I added.

The man stood up slowly. He scratched his head and looked from me to Granny Joss. 'Umm,' he said uncertainly.

At that moment, across the field, a man's voice boomed through a megaphone. '*Mesdames et messieurs, tout est prêt!*' Everyone scrambled in different directions, barging into each other as they ran to do their jobs. A group of men positioned two big cameras directly in front of the hot-air balloon.

Granny Joss and I didn't know what the man had said, but we could hazard a guess – he must be the director, the guy in charge. And seeing as everyone was getting into place, they must be ready to start filming.

'We need to borrow this,' I said to the pilot as I clambered over the top of the wooden basket and dropped down inside next to the propane tank. 'Um, bor-row,' I said slowly. '*Le* 'ot-air balloony. Um, fly?' I shot my hand across the air like a rocket. 'Just for a little bit. Granny Joss?'

I hooked under her elbows and helped her climb into the basket. Tag barked in excitement as he peered over the top of my rucksack. He could sniff an adventure, that dog.

'*Specialiste d'explosives!*' a short man with thick-rimmed glasses cried out, scurrying onto the field. He carried a small box no bigger than a walkie-talkie, with all sorts of silver buttons on it.

Well, even *I* could understand that. Explosives expert? What sort of film *was* this? I turned to the pilot. 'We need to go now, please.' They were gearing up to start filming. If we didn't go now, we might *never* get out of here.

'Here,' Granny Joss said, tugging at a thick brown rope that led over the edge of the basket and was then attached to the ground. 'Give me a hand with this, Matilda.' I raced across to join her, and together we yanked it clean. Bits of grass flew into the air as the rope detached itself and snaked up inside the hot-air balloon. We were lifted slightly off the ground. 'Woah!' I exclaimed, gripping the side of the wicker basket tightly.

The pilot stared at Granny Joss and me, his dark eyebrows knitted together. He opened his mouth to say something.

'Quiet on set!' someone called across the field. 'We've only got one shot to get this right! And where is our star? Where is Philippe—?'

'Ten seconds and counting!' the explosives expert cried, pushing a big silver button on his box.

Granny Joss and I exchanged a look. It was now or never! I motioned to the silver propane tank beside me. 'Go?' I said to the pilot. 'Start engine?'

The pilot looked from me to the cameras and floodlights pointed directly at the hot-air balloon, ready to film. He seemed torn – this all *had* to be part of the script, didn't it?

'Nine, eight—' the explosives expert shouted.

The pilot nodded and turned the wheel of the propane tank, like he was unscrewing a jar of Marmite. A red pipe ran from the tank up into the balloon, where a metal burner was suspended. After a moment, the burner burst into life; an orange flame danced up into the rafters of the canopy.

'Where is Philippe?' the director yelled into the megaphone in panic. '*OÙ EST MON ÉTOILE?*'

'Six, five, four—'

'There he is!!!' a high-pitched scream rang out across the field. 'Philippe!!' Six teenage girls were huddled in a group, all pointing at the hot-air balloon.

'Three, two—'

I frowned at the pilot. What were they all talking about?

BANG!

Tufts of grass and mud shot into the air. The hot-air balloon was knocked sideways and Granny Joss, the pilot and me were thrown across the basket. The metal burner above us roared and a burst of fire shot out of it.

Our ears rang with the noise of the explosion, and dust and smoke filled our eyes. Confusion and panic reigned. A few girls in the crowd started screaming in shock.

I felt a fluttering sensation in my stomach. I was light, as light as air. We were moving upwards. I beamed at Granny Joss. 'This is it! We're off!'

Granny Joss squeezed my shoulder in delight. Even Tag barked appreciatively. Only the pilot seemed disturbed, for he was hanging over the side of the basket, almost falling out of it. Granny Joss grabbed his shirt to hold him back. 'You can't jump! We're too high up!'

On the ground, a chorus of shouts rang out. I swiped away trails of smoke in front of me to take in the scene. In my direct line of sight, I could see trees. The tops of trees. Now blue sky. Now more blue sky. Now clouds. We were on our way!

As we drifted higher, the people down on the ground looked like ants. Every single person – the director, the cameramen, the teenage girls – stared up at us, pointing at the balloon in horror and disbelief.

A thought whizz-popped into my mind. Why would the pilot try to jump from a hot-air balloon? Unless he wasn't a pilot. Unless he was—

'Wait,' I said, my jaw dropping in shock. '*You're* the actor? *You're* the French film star?'

The pilot gripped the sides of the wicker basket so hard his knuckles turned as white as his face. He looked like he was about to throw up, but he managed a weak nod.

'So you can't fly this thing?' I cried, panic working its way up my throat. Miles of French countryside whizzed by as we soared through the air. 'And more importantly,' I added, gulping heavily, 'you can't *land* it?'

Philippe de Bouvier, famous French film star, very much *not* a hot-air balloon pilot, shook his head and slumped down on the floor of the basket, knees tucked up to his chin. He rocked back and forth to comfort himself.

Granny Joss squeezed my shoulder. 'Don't worry, love, it'll all be OK.'

I felt sick. 'That's no comfort, Granny,' I muttered, 'no comfort *whatsoever* seeing as we're very much ABOUT TO DIE!'

Philippe de Bouvier moaned to himself, his eyes rolling up into his head.

But Granny Joss wasn't panicked. She wasn't scared or worried. Instead, she reached past me to fiddle with the valve on the propane tank. 'Oh, I don't think so, dearie,' she said softly. 'I learned how to fly one of these back in the seventies.'

My eyebrows shot up. 'What?'

Granny Joss shrugged, as if this was the sort of thing you do every day. 'I don't like to brag,' she said simply. 'Now sit back and enjoy the ride!'

Wow. My granny knew how to fly a hot-air balloon? And was a properly brilliant scientist? And should have a planet named after her?

As we soared higher and higher, birds flapping past us, France thousands of feet below, I couldn't help but marvel at Granny Joss. I mean, what a gal, right? And that was just the stuff she'd told me about!

17

TWO ARNOS YARMERS IN PARIS

MATILDA MOORE'S FASCINATING FACTS #5

A medium-sized cumulus cloud weighs the same as 80 elephants. (Luckily, clouds can't fall on top of our heads and crush us to death as we go about our daily business. Thanks, gravity!)

Granny Joss and I floated through the clouds above France in a hot-air balloon with a dog and a famous film star for company. It wasn't every day you could say that.

'So, hot-air balloons work,' I said, looking up into the canopy of the balloon, where the flame from the burner danced with life, 'because the air trapped *inside* this balloon is hotter than the air *outside* it.'

Granny Joss nodded as she controlled the propane tank and kept the balloon steady. 'That's right,' she said. 'It's simple physics.'

'It's like an egg floating in salt water,' I continued, remembering the trick Josh had attempted at the science competition the day before. 'An object will float if it's less dense than the water it's floating on, and it'll sink if it's denser. I guess that's what happened to Mickey in the Channel. He *was* pretty dense. So with a hot-air balloon, you need to trap air that's hotter than the air outside, in order to shoot upwards. Hence the burner.'

'You got it,' Granny Joss smiled. 'We simply wrap material round the hot air and we've got ourselves a vehicle.'

'That's incredible,' I said, still amazed at what we were doing.

'It is, Matilda,' Granny Joss said, looking hard at me. Piercing blue eyes searched mine. 'But you're so busy thinking about how things work that you forget to look at where they can take you.' She gestured all around us. 'Admire the view. It's magical up here.'

I peered over the edge of the wicker basket. Miles of beautiful green fields stretched out below us. The sky was about to turn full-on black, and a smattering of lights from farmhouses peppered the view. I'd never seen anything like it before. I'd never even been on a plane.

I delved into my rucksack, taking care to avoid a sleeping Tag, and took out the photographic plate. I held it up and squinted at the stars. 'Which one's Planet Smocks, Granny?' I asked. Granny Joss joined me at the edge of the wicker basket. 'It can't be seen by the naked eye,' she said, pointing upwards. 'But it's in that direction, I think.' She took the glass plate from me and lined it up, so that the blanket of stars could be seen through it.

I shook my head in disbelief. I couldn't believe she'd discovered it. In that moment, more than ever, I knew we *had* to keep going. We *had* to put everything right. 'We can fly all the way to Sweden, can't we?'

Granny Joss nodded. 'That's the plan.'

A plan! At last! We were no longer lost. We didn't need to find the train station or the money for tickets. We could simply fly aaaaaaaaall the way to Stockholm. Probably park the hot-air balloon in the car park of the City Hall too. Make a dramatic entrance to the ceremony, you know, and give Professor Smocks what's what. And nothing, but nothing, could stop us!

'*NON!*' a voice piped up from the floor of the basket.

Philippe de Bouvier. I'd forgotten about him, for he'd stopped rocking and had sat lost in thought for the last half hour while we flew.

'Excuse me?' I said, narrowing my eyes. Who was *he* to interfere with our plan?

Philippe de Bouvier got to his feet and squared up to me. 'I insist that you lond zis plane immediately,' he said in heavily-accented English.

'Hot-air balloon,' Granny Joss corrected.

'Why?' I asked. I spread my arms wide, gesturing at the view. 'It's lovely up here.'

Philippe glared at me. 'Do you know 'oo I am?'

He didn't even wait for me to say, 'Only because some lady in the food queue told us,' or for Granny

Joss to say, more accurately, 'Nope. And we don't give two hoots, either,' before repeating, 'I *insist* that you lond zis plane.'

'Hot-air balloon,' Granny Joss corrected once more. I got the feeling that Philippe wasn't the smartest film star in the world. He was along the lines of Thomas Thomas, if I was being honest. But what *was* perfectly clear was that Philippe de Bouvier was used to getting his own way.

'I am a famoos film staaar,' Philippe stated, as if on cue. 'I've been in ze biggest-grossing movies of all time! In France,' he added, though so quietly I wasn't sure I'd even heard it. 'I own a private yacht, three 'ouses, a Porsche and 'alf a greyhond.'

'What happened to the other half?' I asked.

'*Non*,' Philippe said, starting to get annoyed. 'I own fifty per cent. My sister owns ze other 'alf. We race her.'

'Your sister?' Granny Joss said. I caught the pretend look of innocence on her face. I knew she was teasing him, and enjoying it too.

'The *greyhond*,' Philippe clarified. He was getting more and more frustrated. 'So I am telling you to land this pl— *balloon* now!'

I folded my arms and stared at Philippe de Bouvier firmly. 'Now, listen here,' I said, my voice hard and steady. 'Who cares how famous you are or how much money you make or if you're used to going to film premieres and red carpets and luxury holidays? Who cares if you own a yacht and three mansions and a fancy car and a dog? It's all just – *stuff*. None of it matters. None of it matters as much as flying all the way to Sweden, at any rate.'

Philippe was clearly taken aback by my outburst, for he stared at me in shock. He obviously wasn't used to people arguing with him. But I could see in his eyes that something I'd said had intrigued him. 'Why?' he asked, before he could help himself.

I explained everything as quickly as I could about Professor Smocks's theft and the Nobel Prize ceremony, and I showed him the photographic glass plate. Philippe's jaw dropped lower in astonishment. This was one heck of a story!

When I had finished, he tapped his chin thoughtfully. 'You know,' he said, 'zis would make a wonder-fool movie. Will you sell me ze rights to your life?'

Granny Joss guffawed at that. 'The rights to my life?' she repeated. 'Get away.' She waved her hand at Philippe as if to say, 'Stop that, you total charmer,' but I could tell she was thrilled.

Suddenly, without warning, the hot-air balloon lurched violently to the right. Philippe and the glass plate were thrown across the basket, nearly toppling over the edge of it. 'AAARRRGGGHHH!!!' he yelled, clinging on for dear life. His cries woke Tag, who started yapping immediately at the commotion.

I gripped onto Philippe's shirt and yanked him back into the basket. To be honest, I was more fussed about the glass plate. I placed it carefully back in my rucksack, next to Tag. 'What was that, Granny?'

Granny Joss peered into the top of the canopy. 'We're losing air,' she stated. She kept her voice steady, not wanting to panic anyone, even though the words 'we're losing air' said while travelling thousands of feet above the ground couldn't, in anyone's book, be taken as *good* news.

I squinted upwards and could just about make out a small hole in the canopy, right above the tip of the flame from the burner. A sliver of moonlight shone down through it.

The balloon lurched again, dropping a few feet with a jolt. My stomach fell into my knees at the sudden movement. 'What do we do?' I cried.

Granny Joss grabbed at the rope and tried to pull the balloon to an even keel. 'We land,' she said simply.

I peered down to the ground below. Even with the sudden drop, we were still thousands of feet in the air. And all right, Granny Joss had said she'd learned to fly one of these things back in the 70s, but did she *really* know how to *land* one?

Philippe clutched his head in his hands. 'No, no, no,' he muttered to himself. 'I'm too young to die! I'm too rich! I'm too *famous*! This can't be happening. This cannot be happening, people!'

Granny Joss used all her strength to pull at the rope to keep us steady. I raced to join her, hoping a twelve-year-old's biceps would be better than an eighty-year-old's. A strapping French film star's biceps would have been the *best* option, but Philippe was too panicked to be of much use to anyone.

As I tugged at the rope and peered at the hole in the balloon, a brilliant thought whizz-popped into my head: *The best inventions are those that solve a problem.* A hole had appeared in the canopy and we were hurtling towards the ground. I would need to invent something to cover that hole!

'Turn out your pockets,' I yelled, frantically rummaging through my dungarees for anything I could find. 'A-HA!' I cried, holding up a stick of bubble gum. I quickly unwrapped it and shoved it in my mouth, chewing as fast as I could.

Granny Joss took one hand off the rope and patted her brown trousers down. From her back pocket, she held out a handkerchief and a postage stamp. 'Any good?'

I placed them both in the palm of my hand. 'Philippe?' I asked, turning to him. He was staring into the distance, frozen in fear. 'Philippe!' I gently tugged at his jacket. That seemed to shake him out of his daze. 'What's in your pockets?'

Philippe reached into his leather jacket and pulled out his wallet. From it, he took out a handful of euros. I looked at the notes with longing, tempted to pocket a few. I knew I couldn't, though, not when it was that or death.

I took the euros, the stamp and the handkerchief and fashioned a plaster to stick over the hole in the canopy. I spat out the well-chewed stick of bubble gum and used it as a glue to keep the makeshift plaster together. Finally, I swapped the 'cereal spoon' finger on The Handy-Handy-Hand for the 'catapult' finger and placed the makeshift plaster inside.

I took aim. I knew I only had one shot to get this right. If my catapult flung the hastily-crafted plaster over the edge of the basket, that would be our only hope gone. I squeezed my left eye shut for focus, pressed the button on the palm of The Handy-Handy-Hand and fired.

PING!

The plaster shot up into the canopy and, by some sort of miracle, managed to stick right onto the intended target! The hole was now completely covered by Granny Joss's hankie, the postage stamp, euros and chewed-up bubble gum.

'Go, Matilda!' Granny Joss shouted in delight. 'Nice shot!'

The hot-air balloon evened out almost immediately. Granny Joss adjusted the valve of the metal burner and the balloon floated steadily through the night sky once more.

I reached over and squeezed Granny Joss in a hug. Philippe shook himself from his stupefied state and joined in too. Even Tag leaped up in delight from my rucksack, pawing at my coat. He was probably just hungry, but I took it as a victory dance nonetheless.

'We're saved!' Philippe cried. He burst out laughing. 'I was so panicked! But you did it. We're saved!' He did a funny little jig in delight.

'Hang on a second,' I said, suddenly clocking something. His voice had changed. His words no longer had a French accent to them. Instead, it was something more, well, *English*. 'YOU'RE NOT FRENCH!' I cried, pointing at him accusingly.

Philippe looked shiftily all about him. 'Yes, I am!' he blustered. 'Ah, *oui*.'

'Your accent's gone,' I ploughed on.

'No, it hasn't!' Philippe cried. 'I mean, *non, non*, zis is not true. Zis is all lies, little girl.'

Granny Joss rolled her eyes. 'When you thought we were going to die, you showed your true colours, Philippe.'

Philippe looked between me and Granny Joss for a moment and then let out a deep sigh. 'Fine,' he said eventually. 'I'm actually from . . . Grimsby.'

I didn't know the geography of France very well, but I knew that Grimsby wasn't in it. 'It's a small town up north,' Granny Joss clarified, spotting my confusion. 'Very much in England.'

'My real name's Brian,' Philippe said quietly. His true accent was coming out now – the distinct northern tones no longer hidden. 'Brian Colin Ramsbottom.'

Which was about as far away from Philippe de Bouvier as you could get. I knew it would be cruel to laugh, even though that was what I *really* wanted to do. I mean, RAMSBOTTOM!

'Why the pretence then, Brian?' Granny Joss asked, smiling kindly at him.

'I started acting when I was eighteen,' Philippe – now Brian – confessed. 'But I didn't get any of the roles I auditioned for. All the directors said that "Brian

Ramsbottom from Grimsby" wasn't a star. They didn't give me a chance to show them what I could do. So I moved to France and created moody Philippe de Bouvier, and before I knew it I was getting attention. Everybody wanted me in their films. I became a star.'

'Lots of actors take new names,' Granny Joss said, squeezing Brian's shoulder in support.

'And singers,' I chipped in. 'I don't think Bruno Mars is his real name, you know.'

Brian sighed. 'I feel like such a fraud. But everyone wants Philippe now. No one's going to look twice at Brian Colin Ramsbottom from Grimsby, England.' He leaned back against the wooden basket, lost in thought.

I knew that Brian Ramsbottom was cut up about it, but honestly, it didn't seem like that big a deal. 'Just tell the world who you really are,' I stated matter-of-factly. 'What's the worst that could happen?'

Brian Ramsbottom stared at me, open-mouthed. 'I'd be a laughing stock! No one would employ me ever again! I'd have to sell my houses, the car, the yacht,' he said, reeling it all off on his fingers. 'The dog, *everything*.'

'But you'd be you,' I said simply.

Brian Ramsbottom shook his head mournfully. 'It's not that simple.'

Before I could say, 'Sounds simple enough to me,' a hideous sliding *eeeeccchhhh* noise rang out inside the canopy, followed by the distinct sound of hissing – like a balloon slowly deflating. Which, funnily enough, was exactly what it was.

Granny Joss, Brian Ramsbottom and I peered upwards. The sticky bubble gum that was holding the makeshift plaster in place had come unstuck.

'Action stations!' Granny Joss cried. She moved back to the rope once more, pulling down on it before the balloon even had a chance to go off-kilter.

But it wasn't enough. Not even mine and Brian's weight combined was enough to stop the hot-air balloon from hurtling downwards, zig-zagging its way across the sky as Granny Joss struggled to keep it under control.

I peered over the edge of the basket to see the ground rushing up to meet us. Trees and roofs, the tops of buildings and rivers all whooshed past, growing larger by the second the closer the balloon plunged to the ground.

'We're in Paris!' Brian Ramsbottom called, pointing at various sights as we zoomed over them. '*L'Arc de Triomphe!* The *Notre Dame!* My gosh, there's the Eiffel Tower!'

I didn't think now was the time for a guided tour, but at least if Brian was concentrating on the famous monuments, he wasn't panicking.

'The Eiffel Tower?' Granny Joss repeated. 'That'll do.' She tugged at the valve of the burner and the balloon jolted to the right.

'That'll do for what?' I asked. I had a sinking feeling – and not just from the rapidly deflating hot-air balloon – that I knew exactly where this was going.

The balloon lurched towards the Eiffel Tower. Granny Joss's face scrunched with concentration as she tugged at the rope and the metal burner in turn, manoeuvring the balloon where she wanted it to go.

The ground was now so close I could make out people down below. 'GET OUT OF THE WAY!!' I yelled as loud as I could.

On the bustling streets of Paris, people started looking up and pointing in shock and horror. Was that a hot-air balloon? With – a little girl and an old lady inside? Wait – is that a dog in a rucksack? And—

'PHILIPPE DE BOUVIER!!!' a teenage girl from the large crowd of spectators beneath the Eiffel Tower screamed.

Brian couldn't help himself; he waved and posed for photos as the people down below – tourists queuing for the Eiffel Tower, security guards, Parisian residents hurrying home from work – all took their phones out and started snapping away at him. Brian's movie-star megawatt grin flashed as brightly as the cameras.

The top of the Eiffel Tower was inching closer. The pointy bit at the top. You know, the pointy bit of metal that looks like a giant spike. A giant, metal spike that the hot-air balloon was hurtling towards at speed.

'Easy does it,' Granny Joss muttered as she tugged at the rope. 'Nearly there.'

I grabbed Tag from my rucksack and stuffed him inside my coat to keep him safe. His warm furry body tickled my skin as he wriggled against me and I tried to ignore the pong from his unwashed fur. I clutched the edge of the hot-air balloon basket with both hands.

We were close enough to the ground to hear the gasps and screams from the crowd below. 'Hold on!' I yelled to Brian. He was still busy gurning at his adoring fans.

I squeezed my eyes shut. *I trust you, Granny Joss,* I whispered inside my head. *I trust you.* I could hear the wind whistling in my ears. For one peaceful moment, I imagined this must be what it felt like to fly.

There was a bump. I was thrown halfway across the basket, smacking right into Brian. Someone in the crowd screamed. Tag barked. Granny Joss whistled through her teeth.

And then the strange rhythmic sound of something . . . It took me a moment to work out what it was.

Applause.

People were clapping and whooping and shouting up at us.

I dared to open my eyes. Granny Joss and Brian were smiling at each other. That had to be a good sign. I peered over the edge of the basket. Granny Joss had perched the balloon right on the tip of the Eiffel Tower, without the pointy bit spiking through the wicker basket, impaling us all like a harpoon. Which was nice.

'You did it, Granny!' I cried, hugging her in delight. I forgot I had Tag in my coat, and he yelped as we crushed him in our embrace.

'We're saved!' Brian cried in sheer relief. He let out a low whistle. 'You know, I swear I saw my life flashing before my eyes. But now, this,' he said, gesturing all around us, '*surviving*, it's like I've been given a second chance in life. And I'm going to be true to myself. I'm going to be Brian Colin Ramsbottom once more.' He heartily slapped Granny Joss on the back. 'Top bird for getting us here safely.' He looked over the edge of the basket. 'I mean, it's a bit wonky, but it'll do.'

The hot-air balloon was indeed listing to one side on top of the Eiffel Tower, like a sinking ship, but I didn't think Brian was in *any* position to complain about Granny Joss's parking. 'Hey,' I said, slightly miffed. '*You* try landing a hot-air balloon.'

Just at that moment, a voice rang out. It was amplified, as if coming through a loudspeaker or a megaphone. '*RESTEZ OÙ VOUS ÊTES!*' it boomed.

Granny Joss and I looked to one another in panic. 'What did they say?' I whispered.

Brian Ramsbottom smiled at us. 'They said, "Welcome to Paris," he cried, his arms spread wide. 'Rightly so. How polite.'

'But they sounded foot-stompingly angry,' I said.

The voice blared through the megaphone again. '*RESTEZ OÙ VOUS ÊTES! NOUS SOMMES LA POLICE.*'

I recognized *one* of those words. Granny Joss peered over the edge of the basket. When she turned back to me and Brian, her eyebrows were so far up her forehead, I had to suppress the urge to giggle at her startled face. 'There's tons of them,' she hissed.

'Police?' I guessed.

'*Armed* police,' Granny Joss gulped.

I imagined that *most* policemen had arms – two, hopefully – but I knew what Granny Joss was getting at. You didn't become *that* shocked at tons of policemen with two arms. You became *that* shocked when tons of policemen were pointing guns at you.

'*MAINS EN L'AIR!*' the voice boomed. And then adding, this time in English, just in case: 'We're coming up!'

Below us, the sound of hundreds of feet thundered on the steps. Through the criss-cross metal structure of the Eiffel Tower, a single file of policemen, dressed all in black, with peaked caps on their heads and rifles in their hands, pounded up the narrow set of stairs that led to a platform just below where the hot-air balloon perched.

Beads of sweat gathered on my forehead. We hadn't actually done anything wrong, had we? Landing a hot-air balloon on the pointy bit of the Eiffel Tower wasn't something we'd set out to do. We were improvising!

The armed police did *not* see it that way.

Granny Joss, Brian Ramsbottom and me all thrust our hands in the air as the head of the armed police stepped onto the platform below us. I wasn't one to scare easily, but I had to admit, seeing a hundred-odd policemen staring up at us with guns in their hands made me a *smidge* nervous.

'We don't want any trouble,' Granny Joss called. 'We just want to get down and then we'll be on our way.'

'Unless you fancy taking us to Sweden,' I chipped in. It was worth a shot.

Brian Ramsbottom flashed us a toothy grin. 'Leave this to me,' he said dramatically. 'Gentlemen,' he called, leaning down over the edge of the basket. 'And one lady. Allow me to explain.'

He ran his hand through his hair and launched into an impassioned speech about our mission to Stockholm, and how he'd been on *such* a journey in the last few hours – not just geographically, even though we'd flown hundreds of miles in the hot-air balloon, but spiritually too. And he knew now that he had to be Brian Colin Ramsbottom once more. He had to be true to himself as an actor and an artist and a son of Grimsby.

Unfortunately, what Brian Colin Ramsbottom did *not* know was that he couldn't speak a word of French. No matter that he'd lived and worked in

France for several years, he'd never actually mastered the language. He never gave interviews and he barely spoke to people on set, pretending he was terribly shy. I guess that's how he'd got away with it for so long.

What he had actually said to the armed police when passionately delivering his speech was:

'*Many monkeys ago, seventeen bicycles went fishing. I angry like purple, but rainbows are funny, don't you mind? But I, Philippe de Bouvier, chocolate mousepad and twelve years of headphones, laugh as babies sleep. Brian Colin Ramsbottom is forty million cheeses and "ACTION!" and red pens because moon cycles have washing machines.*'

The armed police looked to one another in confusion. A few at the back started muttering to each other, for they *thought* they recognized this guy – wasn't he that actor? But what on earth was he banging on about? And what was he doing in a hot-air balloon with an old lady and a little girl with a dog stuffed down her coat on top of the Eiffel Tower? No one could quite understand *what* was going on.

After a moment, the policeman in charge called up to us once more. 'Get down 'ere zis second,' he demanded. 'And I'm warning you. No funny bizness.'

Granny Joss, Brian Ramsbottom and I all looked at one another, wide-eyed.

How were we going to talk our way out of this?

18
BRIAN'S BIG ANNOUNCEMENT

1165 miles to Stockholm

MATILDA MOORE'S FASCINATING FACTS #6

The Eiffel Tower was built for the 1889 Paris Exhibition but wasn't intended to be permanent. (Good job it was, else we wouldn't have had anything to land our hot-air balloon on. Apart from the ground. With a SPLAT!)

There are 20,000 light bulbs illuminating the Tower. Go, Thomas Edison! (All of them were lit up when we descended. Imagine the electricity bills! And Dad moans at *me* for leaving my bedroom light on through the night!)

There are 1665 steps leading from the top to the bottom (and Brian Colin Ramsbottom moaned the WHOLE way down. Honestly, he was terrified of its height. Never mind that he'd spent the past few hours inside a hot-air balloon, thousands of feet above the ground, let alone having hurtled towards a near-death disaster. Actors, hey?).

After an extraceedingly slow descent down the Eiffel Tower, we finally reached the bottom. The crowd that was gathered there burst into applause again. The armed police that were waiting for us did not. 'You need to come with us,' the head of the armed guard said.

We didn't have time for this. Tag agreed, for he wriggled around inside my coat, making small growling sounds and snapping his jaws. 'Shhh, Tag,' I soothed. 'You can't bite them.' Even though that was *exactly* what I wanted him to do.

What we needed was a distraction. An idea whizz-popped into my head. The Exploding Bag Trick! I'd seen it on the internet a million times. You put vinegar and bicarbonate of soda into a sandwich bag and watch as the mixture expands until the bag goes pop! It makes you jump every time. The police would be so spooked they wouldn't notice us sneaking off. The only snag was that we didn't have a sandwich bag. Or vinegar. Or bicarbonate of soda. Oh, why didn't I think to pack *that* into my rucksack? Maybe I could just make the 'pop' noises?

Granny Joss placed a hand on my arm, sensing my distress. 'It'll be all right, love,' she soothed. I let out a sigh. There was nothing for it but to turn ourselves in.

But just at that moment, Brian Ramsbottom bustled forward. 'There's something I'd like to say,' he boomed in his natural Grimsby accent.

A few eyebrows shot up in the crowd, but all eyes turned to stare at him. 'I have an announcement to make to the world,' Brian declared dramatically.

Obviously thinking they were going to get some juicy gossip, Brian's fans surged forward. The crowd surrounded us, jostling Granny Joss and me. Flashes from cameras shone into our faces.

'*RESTEZ OÙ VOUS ÊTES!*' the head of the armed police cried. He clearly thought this was 'funny bizness'.

The crowd ignored him. 'What is it, Philippe?' someone shouted.

As the tourists and spectators crowded around us, hanging on Brian's every word, Brian turned to Granny Joss and me and whispered, 'Go. Now.'

'What?' I hissed.

'While I've got their attention,' he ploughed on, nodding to the crowd. 'Slip away. You *must* get to Sweden! I'll take the flak.'

'We can't let you do that,' Granny Joss said. She looked from Brian to the armed police and back again.

The eyes of France's former number one film star filled with tears. 'I insist you do,' he whispered. 'It's because of you I feel able to be myself again. I'll never be able to repay you for giving me Brian Colin Ramsbottom back.'

I was about to say, 'Actually, Brian, you *could* repay us. Give us a few euros to get to Sweden,' when he hissed once more, 'Go! Hurry! And good luck!'

He gave a big sniff and turned back to the crowd. 'Ladies and gentlemen,' he cried. 'I am delighted to announce that I have reached a new phase in my career.'

'You're retiring from acting?' someone called.

'Thank goodness,' shouted another.

'No,' Brian replied, suppressing his annoyance. 'I'm not retiring.'

As all eyes were on Brian, with everyone – including half of the armed guards – waiting with bated breath to hear what he'd say, Granny Joss and I, clutching Tag tightly through my coat, slowly, ever so slowly, shuffled a few steps backwards.

The armed guards didn't seem to notice. So we shuffled a few more. And then a few more—

'My announcement is—' Brian declared.

The crowd swarmed closer, surrounding him, and Granny Joss and I ducked down and weaved through the huddled mass.

'I'm English!' Brian Colin Ramsbottom cried.

No one said anything at that. The crowd looked to one another in confusion.

'My real name is Brian Colin Ramsbottom,' he ploughed on.

Granny Joss and I burst out of the crowd and raced down whatever French street we were on, Tag's body bouncing around inside my coat, our feet pounding on the cobbles as we hurtled round the corner.

I glanced back over my shoulder. The armed police were still encircling the tourists, who were still encircling Brian, and *everyone* looked as if they didn't have a clue what was happening.

'I'm still me!' Brian called, his voice carrying on the wind to us. 'I'm just the same as Philippe! Except not French. Or moody. I'm actually pretty jolly, really.'

Granny Joss and I hurried through the backstreets of Paris, past clothes shops that were pulling their shutters down for the evening, past cafes that were still serving coffees to the brave tourists sitting outside. We ran as quickly as Granny Joss's eighty-year-old legs could take us, trying to put as much distance between us and the armed policemen as possible. I clutched at my coat, hoping Tag wasn't getting too jostled around inside it.

After a few minutes, Granny Joss drew to a stop and leaned against the nearest wall as she took a deep breath. 'Are you all right, Granny?' I asked, remembering Dad's comments about her tired legs. I really hoped all this exercise wasn't too much for her.

Granny Joss spotted a bench across the street. 'I don't know about you,' she said wearily, 'but I could do with a sit-down.' She staggered across the road towards it.

I felt so guilty McGuilty at that. I knew how exhausted *I* was, so how shattered must Granny Joss be?

'Ooof,' she said, exhaling loudly as she lowered herself onto the bench. 'It's nice to take the weight off.' She closed her eyes, allowing herself to relax.

I slung my rucksack down by my feet and sat beside her in stunned silence, processing everything that had happened in the last few hours. I checked my watch. It was 7.13 p.m., which meant 8.13 p.m. French time. It felt like midnight – it had been that long a day. My stomach growled again. It had been an *awfully* long time since we had been on Chris P and Svetlanka's boat crossing the Channel, eating biscuits and cake.

'Cake!' I cried, the word popping into my head. I stuffed my hand in my coat pocket and pulled out the slab of cake that Svetlanka had thrust at me as we were saying goodbye in Calais.

I unwrapped the cake from the clingfilm and enjoyed the sensation of my stomach easing its rumbling as I nibbled on it. Tag, smelling food from a mile off, started yapping, so I tore off a small chunk and dropped it inside my coat. He wriggled around as he ate, his fur tickling my skin.

We were streets away from the Eiffel Tower, but I could still see it in the distance, all lit up in its magnificent glory. A few of the police guards were at the top of the platform, debating how to get the hot-air balloon down from its wonky perch.

Bright lights puckered the night sky in all directions. I could see why so many people came here on their holidays, for it was a truly beautiful city.

As I took in the sights, Granny Joss rested her eyes and Tag nestled snugly inside my coat. Then an elderly woman approached the bench. I wouldn't have taken any notice of her, had she not been acting so strangely.

The woman was smaller than Granny Joss, but she was roughly the same age and had the exact same shock of frizzy white hair. She hovered near our bench, clutching a black briefcase, and looked all about her nervously. *How odd,* I thought to myself. I carried on nibbling the cake, taking in the sights and enjoying the peace and quiet.

After a moment, Granny Joss's eyes snapped open. 'Iwasn'tasleepIwasjustrestingmyeyes,' she mumbled, all in one go. She sounded both sleepy *and* guilty McGuilty.

'Look, Granny,' I whispered, motioning to the woman as subtly as I could. 'There's a lady who looks like you.'

Granny Joss leaned past me. 'Where?'

'Behind me.'

Granny Joss looked again and then shook her head. 'There's no one there.'

I whipped round and was just about to say, 'I think you need glasses, Granny,' when I realized the lady had vanished. 'How strange. She was right there.'

'Oh well,' Granny Joss sighed. 'It doesn't matter.' She looked at me, blue eyes twinkling. 'What does is that we've had *quite* the adventure already, Matilda. Let's think about how we're going to get to Sweden, shall we? Preferably incident-free.'

I held out the hunk of cake to Granny Joss, but she shook her head. So I re-wrapped it in the clingfilm and shoved it back in my pocket. I counted on my fingers. We had sixteen hours now to get to Stockholm before the Nobel Prize ceremony the next day. We *certainly* didn't have time for unforeseen escapades.

'OK,' I agreed. 'No more unexpected adventures.'

Which was a very unfortunate thing to have said. The timing couldn't have been worse. For at that moment, Granny Joss and I both felt something prod into our backs. 'Don't move,' a voice growled in Granny Joss's ear.

I tried to spin round to see what was going on, but whatever was against my back was pressed harder into it. 'Get up,' the voice hissed.

Well, that was just confusing. 'But you said "don't move",' I stated.

'Don't be smart with me. Get up!' The voice belonged to a man, speaking in broken English.

Granny Joss and I looked at one another in panic. She nodded and both of us slowly got to our feet and turned around to see a burly, bald man in a suit pointing a gun at us.

I gulped. Having gone through twelve whole years of life with nothing of the sort happening, for the second time in *that very hour*, I'd had a gun pointed at me. I *really* didn't want this to become a habit.

'Wh-what do you want with us?' Granny Joss asked. I could tell she was as nervous as I was.

The man waved his gun towards a sleek silver car with blacked-out windows parked up on the kerb. 'Get in,' he demanded, his voice flat and lifeless.

Tag growled inside my coat. I had half a mind to tell him to bite, just this once. Instead, I grabbed my rucksack. 'Where are we going?'

The man's lips curled into a sneer. 'Rulenska isn't very happy with you,' he smirked. He had a huge scar on his cheek. I didn't even want to think about how he got it.

But ... Rulenska? I didn't know anyone called that. It was far too exotic-sounding for Arnos Yarm.

The brute opened the back door of the car and bundled Granny Joss and me inside. I couldn't help thinking that we could have done with the armed police after all.

We slid onto the back seat. The burly man thrust his hand in my face, hairy knuckles inches from my nose. 'Phone,' he barked.

'Wh-what?'

'Give me your phone,' he sneered. 'Don't pretend you haven't got one.'

I dug in my dungarees for my mobile, fishing it out and handing it to the thug. I dreaded to think how many missed calls I'd had from my parents. I felt a pang, then. If only Mum and Dad knew where we were and what was happening.

The man clicked his fingers at Granny Joss. 'Phone,' he repeated.

'Oh, she definitely hasn't got one,' I said. 'I tried to make her get one, because then I could use it when I visit her at Canterbury Cares – that's her care home.' I knew I was babbling, but I couldn't stop, I was so nervous. 'Mum and Dad won't let me get a good one, you know, one with the internet on, because they think I'd run up a phone bill the size of your—'

'Enough!' the man with the gun cried, holding up his hand. 'Stop talking.' He huffed as he opened the passenger door and got in. He said a few brief words to the driver, but I couldn't hear what.

The burly man shot us a final glance, before pressing the button that raised a glass partition between the front and back seats. 'Hey!' I shouted, leaning forward and banging on the glass. It didn't have any effect. The glass may have been see-through, but it was completely soundproof. I tried the door handle, rattling it desperately. No such luck.

'We're trapped!' I cried as the car screeched away from the kerb and into the evening Parisian traffic. I gulped. Who knew who this Rulenska woman was, or what she was going to do with us?!

Granny Joss patted my hand soothingly. 'It'll be all right, love,' she said softly. 'We've got each other.' She looked out of the window, lost in thought. 'Everything will be all right in the end,' she whispered. 'And if it's not all right, well then, it's not the end. Wilf used to say that. We saw it in a film.'

I was glad *somebody* was keeping calm. I smoothed Tag on the head and said, 'It's all right, boy. It'll be all right.' I was saying it more for myself, really. I didn't want to appear scared in front of Granny Joss, not when she'd saved us from death by expertly landing a rapidly-deflating hot-air balloon.

But as I looked through the car's blacked-out windows at the bustling streets of Paris rushing past, with their bright lights and sounds, not knowing where we were headed or what awaited us when we got there, I couldn't help the fluttering feeling in my tummy. I couldn't help longing for home, wishing I was with my parents on one of our boring road trips to the parking ticket museum in Kent, with their slogan 'You'll Have A Fine Time!', and *not* in the back of a car with a man pointing a gun at us.

19

DESPERATE TIMES

I loved my parents, but they were very unadventurous people. We went to the supermarket every Saturday to do the Big Shop, and after all the essentials had been shoved in the trolley, we were all allowed one treat each. Whereas I would buy a *National Geographic* magazine one week, a pack of Wagon Wheels or some big plastic comedy glasses the next, my parents *always* chose the same thing.

Mum: a pack of lavender-scented tissues. She liked to place them in drawers, cabinets, the car's glove box, my rucksack and, bizarrely once, the fridge. Mum didn't think anyone should be more than a three-second-dive away from a tissue, cos you never knew when you'd be in need of one.

Dad: a box of figs.

Every week. Always the same.

But desperate times called for desperate measures.

Knowing Granny Joss and I were alive, thanks to my text message, but unable to get to speak to me despite constant phone calls, Dad knew it was time to take matters into their own hands.

My parents spent all morning scouring the streets of Arnos Yarm before heading to Dover, waiting to see if we turned up. We didn't, obviously. So they'd driven home again, picked up their passports and some provisions, and were on board the ferry to France within the hour.

My parents had never done anything like this before. They were mad at me for running away, although they had to admit, deep down – like extraceedingly deep down, past their stomachs and guts and undigested bits of porridge from breakfast – a teensy part of them found it all highly exciting. This must be what it felt like to live life on the edge!

But still . . . as the ferry sailed across the Channel, Mum and Dad stood on the deck, gazing out at the fading lights of the port of Dover, and wondered where on earth their little girl had got to.

20

OVER THE BORDER

690 miles to Stockholm

Their little girl was in the back of a car driven by a man pointing a gun at her.

Before Granny Joss had fallen asleep, she'd said, 'Take your coat off, else you won't feel the benefit,' like the grandmother she is, and so here Tag was, nestled inside the front pocket of my dungarees like a baby kangaroo in a pouch. There was something comforting about his scraggly body against me, like the hot-water bottle Mum places in my bed to keep me snug on a winter's night like this. I didn't know if Tag had an owner, but they hadn't looked after him particularly well. I'd probably done him a favour, taking him in.

We'd been driving for a couple of hours. The bright streets of Paris had given way to back roads and countryside. There had been a moment, not long ago, when the car had stopped at a checkpoint, but we were waved through, no questions asked. We must have crossed some sort of border and were now driving through Belgium. Or Germany. Or Luxembourg. Or, if it had really gone wrong, onto a cargo ship headed for Belize.

I closed my eyes, trying to take it all in. On the one hand, I was *terrified* that we were heading towards certain death. But on the other, if Rulenska had *wanted* us killed for some reason, surely the man in the suit could have done it in Paris? Unless Rulenska wanted to do it in person.

I allowed my whizz-popping mind to go blank. I was utterly exhausted. I may as well follow Granny Joss's lead and sleep while I could.

I awoke with a jolt. For three glorious seconds, I was back home in Arnos Yarm, in my comfy bed with the picture of Einstein on the duvet cover. Then I remembered what had happened.

I wiped sleep out of my eyes and peered through the window. We were in a city. Tall buildings loomed over us as we drove through traffic-clogged streets. Skyscrapers sat alongside medieval churches; the sounds from bars and restaurants filled my ears as people stumbled out of them into the night.

We stopped outside a sharp-angled apartment building made entirely of glass. A man in a top hat opened the door for us. I gently shook Granny Joss awake and helped her out of the car. I checked my watch – 11.37 p.m. 12.37 a.m. in French time. If we were even still in France.

The burly man with the gun had put his gun away, but nevertheless scowled menacingly as he ushered us into the apartment block. Our shoes clacked on the marble floor. Fancy artwork adorned the walls. This was one classy establishment, wherever we were. I've never been to The Ritz, but I reckon that would have looked like a rundown B&B compared to this.

I groped for Granny Joss's hand as we were nudged into the lift at the back of the lobby. The lift travelled all the way to the top of the building, marking our stop with a PING! 'The penthouse suite,' the burly thug said in his gruff voice.

The lift opened onto the most magnificent room I'd ever seen. Black-and-white tiles on the floor. A grand piano in the corner. Floor-to-ceiling windows ran the entire length of the suite, offering the most stunning view of whatever city we were in.

And sitting in front of the window in an egg-shaped chair was a glamorous woman. She had flame-red hair, with matching red lipstick and nails, and wore a slinky black dress with an enormous sparkling diamond brooch on her shoulder.

She looked familiar somehow, though we'd obviously never met before. This must be Rulenska. And her cat – for sitting in her lap was a fluffy white bundle of fur, licking its paws and looking at us with lazy amber eyes.

'Doctor Françoise Bertrand,' Rulenska said in a heavily-accented voice. 'I've been expecting you—'

Before she could finish her sentence, the cat leaped off her lap and bounded over towards me. 'Kosovo!' Rulenska called, startled.

Tag nestled down further against my chest, growling softly. He didn't like the look of the cat. I couldn't blame him. I didn't like the look of the cat's owner. 'Shhh!' I soothed as the cat weaved in and out of my legs.

Granny Joss stepped forward, taking the opportunity to appeal to Rulenska. 'I feel I should tell you,' she offered, 'there's been some sort of misunderstanding. I'm not Doctor Françoise whoever you're after. I'm Professor Joss Moore. And this is my granddaughter, Matilda.'

Rulenska peered at us both curiously. She took in Granny Joss's white hair. 'Where's the briefcase?' she said after a moment, her voice silky smooth.

'What briefcase?' Granny Joss asked, surprised.

Something in my brain clicked. 'There was *another* old lady,' I said slowly, putting it all together, 'who was standing near us, just before he got us.' I nodded to the man with the gun. 'She looked just like Granny Joss. And *she* was carrying a briefcase.'

Rulenska arched an eyebrow like she didn't believe me. 'So where are my diamonds?' she sighed.

'Diamonds?' I whispered. I had to admit this was *highly* intriguing. 'What diamonds?'

'I'm a diamond dealer,' Rulenska stated matter-of-factly. 'The best in the business, so I know when I'm being double-crossed. A batch of my diamonds went missing last week and I got wind that one of my rivals, Doctor Françoise Bertrand, was involved.'

The penny dropped. 'So you caught Granny Joss thinking she was Doctor Bertrand,' I said, seeing where she'd gone wrong. A wave of relief washed over me. 'Well, now you know she's not and it's all just a terrible mix-up, you can let us go!'

Rulenska let out a tinkly little laugh. 'I don't think so,' she said. 'Even if you are who you say you are, you'll have to be dealt with. You know too much.'

'But you're the one who *told* us everything!' I yelled. 'We wouldn't have known *anything* if you'd not told us!'

'You know where I live,' Rulenska shrugged. 'You could go to the authorities. I have people looking for me.' She cleared her throat. 'I *may* not do *all* of my dealings in line with the law, you see.'

'We won't!' I cried. 'Just let us go!'

But Rulenska didn't care. She turned on her heel and walked to the window, staring at the view like she didn't have a single worry in the world. Never mind the fact she'd just ordered two people to be murdered.

'No!' I shrieked. 'This isn't fair!'

All the while, I couldn't shake the feeling that I'd met Rulenska before. Oh, where did I know her from? She looked so familiar.

Behind me, I heard the click of the gun's safety catch being taken off. Granny Joss squeezed her eyes tightly. 'I love you, Matilda,' she whispered.

MATILDA MOORE'S FASCINATING FACTS #7

The human brain takes in 11 million bits of information every second, but is only aware of 40.

(I knew the answer was in my mind somewhere. I just had to think. Our lives depended on it.)

From out of nowhere, from the very back of my brain, just when the chips were down, I had a flash of inspiration: Kosovo the cat. Rulenska's familiar-looking face. Rulenska's familiar-sounding name.

Yazooks! I'd got it!

'Svetlanka!' I cried.

The man in the suit stopped in his tracks as Rulenska gasped in shock. She spun round to face me. 'That's my sister!' she whispered. 'How did you—?'

'We were on her boat this morning!' I shouted. 'She brought us from Dover to Calais, with her husband Chris P Duck.'

Rulenska frowned at that. 'Crispy Duck?' She stared at me and Granny Joss, unable to take it all in. 'No,' she said after a moment. 'This cannot be true. You could have made that up after finding me on the internet. It's a ploy to save yourselves.'

'He's got my mobile!' I yelled, pointing to the brute. 'And I don't even have the internet on it!'

Rulenska clicked her fingers at her henchman. 'Show me the photo of Doctor Bertrand,' she demanded.

From inside his suit jacket, the brute pulled out a grainy photo of an elderly lady with frizzy white hair walking down a street. It was hard to see her face properly. Rulenska looked at it, then at Granny Joss and back again. I could tell she was torn.

'You have to believe us,' I pleaded. 'We know your sister! Svetlanka told us all about coming over from Kosovo. That you and she were separated after your parents divorced. She was so nice. She gave us tea and custard creams and—'

I gasped as I remembered something. Of course! As quickly as I could, I whipped out the slab of cake from my pocket and held it out to Rulenska. 'Grandmama Olga's easy-peasy-lemon-and-orange-marmalade-and-leftover-bits-of-old-tea-bag fruit cake!'

Rulenska clutched the back of her chair for support as I thrust the cake at her. She peeled back a corner of the clingfilm and nibbled on the cake. After a moment, tears welled up in her eyes – the taste taking her back to her childhood. 'I can't – I can't believe it,' she whispered.

She took a deep breath and then seized Granny Joss and me by the elbow and guided us to a pristine glass dining table on the other side of the room. 'You've come such a long way,' she said, beaming at both of us. 'You must be hungry. I want to hear *everything* while we eat.'

And that's how Granny Joss, Tag and I narrowly avoided being murdered by one of Europe's Most Wanted Criminals. Which was nice.

As we told Rulenska all about our mission to Sweden, and about how Tag had led us to Chris P Duck's boat in the first place, she ordered a series of delicious dishes to be brought out. Granny Joss and I wolfed down everything, including:

Sauerkraut

Knödel

Fischbrötchen

Bratwurst

Currywurst (that was the worst)

And . . . hamburgers. 'The national dish,' Rulenska laughed. 'It's all I've eaten since we left France.'

My ears pricked up at that. 'Hamburg!' I cried. 'You drove us to Germany?'

Rulenska nodded. 'I'm lying low here for a while,' she whispered. 'Just until some trouble in France blows over.'

Never mind that, I thought. We were still on track for Stockholm!

Now just the small matter of how to get there.

'Do you think,' I asked shyly – for even though Rulenska had provided a feast for us, she was, after all, a master criminal who had been about to murder us – 'you could have your car drop us at the station? And maybe lend us some euros? We could see if there's an overnight train to Sweden.'

Rulenska smiled. She leaned down and patted Kosovo under the table, where he was merrily sharing a whole plate of pellkartoffeln with Tag. 'I can do better than that,' Rulenska purred. 'I'll have you taken all the way there.'

'Really?' Granny Joss asked. 'That's ever so kind.'

Rulenska shrugged, as if it meant nothing, but I could see how visibly moved she was. 'Thank you for giving me such wonderful memories of my grandmama and news of my long-lost sister,' she whispered.

The man with the gun who had, in fact, put his gun away an hour ago, once this whole mix-up over Granny Joss and Doctor Bertrand had been straightened out, stepped forward and spoke to Rulenska in French.

'Yes, yes,' Rulenska said briskly, waving him away with her hand. She turned to Granny Joss and me once more. 'He says I have a prior engagement,' she sighed. This man must be Rulenska's bodyguard, hitman and the guy in charge of her diary. I really didn't envy him. 'It's at the circus, as a matter of fact,' Rulenska stated, an idea forming. 'Would you like to come?'

I pushed my plate away from me, suppressed a belch that was working its way up from my stomach, and said, 'Thanks, Rulenska, but we're keen to get on. Just in case anything else goes wrong.' The phrase 'unexpected adventures' popped into my head.

Rulenska checked her watch. 'You won't need to leave yet. I'll have my driver take you through the early hours. My missing diamonds are still out there, and I need to talk to my associate.'

'At the circus?' I asked, confused.

Rulenska scraped back her chair and scooped Kosovo into her arms. 'I'll soon have you on your way.'

Granny Joss shrugged at me in a 'what can we do?' manner. It was true — we couldn't get to Sweden without Rulenska's help. We'd have to go along with it.

And at least we'd be arriving at the Nobel Prize ceremony in a stylish silver car, without having to worry about parking a hot-air balloon. *And* we were no longer going to be murdered by an angry Kosovan gangster. *And* I'd eaten a whole stack of burgers FOR FREE!

Things were looking up.

21

ROLL UP! ROLL UP!

I'd never been to the circus before, let alone an open-all-night one. Mum and Dad thought that watching clowns throw custard pies in each other's faces wasn't particularly educational, you see.

The circus was in a big field on the outskirts of Hamburg. Various tents of different colours and sizes were dotted all around, along with caravans where the performers lived, cages where the animals were housed, and stalls where food and drinks were dished out.

Rulenska had put Kosovo on a lead and had given me one for Tag too, which meant he could trot alongside us without me worrying about him running off and causing no end of trouble. No one said anything as we moved through the crowds, as odd as the sight of a cat on a lead might be. Everyone seemed to know who Rulenska was and what she was capable of. I couldn't help but gulp as we trailed behind her. I shared a look with Granny Joss as we were shown to our seats – naturally the best in the house – and knew she was thinking the same thing.

The lights dimmed and Granny Joss and I watched in wonder as the clowns performed their routine, carrying a plank of wood between them, knocking each other around the head, showering a bucket of glitter on the crowd. Next up were the trapeze artists and tightrope walkers who performed their marvellous routines fifty feet in the air, never once wavering. I knew from our hot-air balloon adventure how scary being that high up could be, let alone trying to walk on a tightrope.

My absolute favourite, though, was the contortionist. A hush descended as one of the clowns brought on a suitcase. After a moment, with everyone wondering what was going on, the suitcase started rattling. Slowly, very slowly, as we all leaned forward to get a closer look, the suitcase unzipped. From it, a leg appeared. And then another, and then two arms, a torso and a head. The contortionist unfolded herself and stood up to rapturous applause. She bowed, and her leotard, bejewelled with stones, sparkled in the darkness.

My hands were numb from clapping. I looked at Granny Joss and a warm feeling spread through me as I saw how happy she was. It sure beat doing jigsaw puzzles at the care home. If nothing else, if we got to Sweden and there was NO WAY of wiping the smug smile off Professor Smocks's face or getting him to admit that he had stolen Granny Joss's research, well, at least I had given her a terrific adventure. A terrific, unexpected adventure, consisting of milk floats, ferries, hot-air balloons, famous film stars, armed police and now this – a show of lions and clowns and elephants and a bejewelled, bendy contortionist at one o'clock in the morning.

Even better, after the show had finished and Rulenska headed off for her meeting with the ringmaster, Granny Joss, Tag and I were invited backstage to see the animals and performers. We walked through the back flap of the big tent and into an even more amazing space. Backstage, it turned out, was where the *real* show happened.

Fire-eaters chatted to men on stilts and gymnasts munched on burgers while drummers banged their bongos next to them. The trapeze artist fed the elephant a bag of peanuts. A group of ladies practised sword-swallowing in a corner. Granny Joss didn't think I should join in with that.

At that moment, an almighty 'ROOOAAARRR!' thundered across the field. Granny Joss and I looked at each other in sheer delight *and* sheer terror. 'The lions!' I whispered. I hoped they weren't free to roam backstage like the other performers.

Another 'ROOOAAAARRR!!!!'

Tag leaped up into my arms. I smuggled him back inside my coat, stuffing his lead in my pocket.

'Is that lion all right?' Granny Joss asked the nearest person. 'He sounds rather agitated.' The nearest person, unfortunately, was a mime artist in a black-and-white stripy outfit and black beret. He shrugged unhelpfully.

Before anyone could ask any more questions, a clown ran into the backstage area, his hands waggling above his head in despair. 'Someone call a vet!' he yelled in a German accent. 'Samson's dying! We can't lose him. He's the star of the show and we all love him!'

Granny Joss placed a hand gently on his arm. 'Take me to him,' she said. I was as surprised as the clown. 'I was married to a vet for fifty-five years,' Granny Joss explained. 'I picked up a thing or two.'

The clown looked about him for backup. 'Uh,' he stuttered. 'I'm not sure you should—'

Granny Joss drew herself up to her full height and hugged her red coat round her. 'My name is Professor Jocelyn Moore, FRS, FRSE, FRAS. Astrophysicist, *Times* Crossword Champion of the Year 1987, full clean driving licence, and a fully-subscribed member of the RSPCA.'

I had to admit – I was no longer surprised by her revelations. I guess you could cram a lot into eighty years.

The clown's jaw dropped in shock. After a moment, he shook himself and stuck out his hand. 'I'm Frederick,' he said. 'Come with me.' He led Granny Joss through the backstage area. I hurried after them, my rucksack bouncing up and down on my shoulders, Tag bouncing up and down inside my coat.

At the back of the field were two huge iron cages, each housing a fully-grown, golden-maned, utterly magnificent lion. One was lying on the ground, lazily licking his paws, tail swatting the air. He looked on in mild curiosity as we approached the cages. I didn't like the thought of animals all cooped up, but still – I prayed that the metal was extra-strength.

The other lion was lying on the floor, listless and dopey-looking. His mouth was wide open, white froth foaming round his lips.

Granny Joss took one look and said, 'We need to sedate him if I am to examine him. Do you have any tranquillizers?' Frederick retrieved a box beside the cage. From it, he pulled out a massive flare gun, and loaded a long cylindrical dart into it.

I was about to say, 'Are you sure you should let a *clown* shoot the lion?' when Granny Joss lifted the gun from him, put her left eye to the eyepiece and squeezed the trigger. I mentally noted that 'gamekeeper' and 'crack shot' could be added to her list of accomplishments.

The tranquillizer dart sank into the lion's leg, and within mere moments he was fast asleep. Granny Joss propped the gun beside the cage and motioned for Frederick to open it. She was going in.

MATILDA MOORE'S FASCINATING FACTS #8

An individual blood cell takes 60 seconds to make a complete circuit of your body.

(As Granny Joss crept inside the lion's cage, *all* of my blood cells rushed straight to my ears. Sleeping lion or not, this was risky.)

Frederick quietly turned the key in the lock and the cage door sprang open. At that moment, my phone buzzed. I pulled out my mobile from my pocket and saw 'DAD' flash on the screen. I didn't know how long I could keep putting him off. It wasn't fair to let Mum and Dad think Granny Joss and I were lost, or dead, or something.

With a heavy heart, I pressed 'ACCEPT'. 'Hello?'

'Matilda!' Dad cried. I heard the relief in his voice, and immediately felt guilty McGuilty that I hadn't spoken to him before now. 'Where are you?'

'Um,' I said, looking at Granny Joss kneeling next to a lion. 'It's – complicated.'

'Are you all right?' Dad asked.

I looked at the lion again. 'Yep,' I said, trying to keep my voice steady.

'Just tell us where you are, love,' Dad said.

'At the circus. In Hamburg.'

It was at that moment that Dad's voice changed. 'Now look here, Matilda,' Dad huffed down the phone. He didn't appreciate me lying, even though I wasn't. 'You'd better stop this messing around and tell us where you are.'

'I already said!' I protested. 'Granny Joss is looking after one of the lions and—'

'Don't lie to me, young lady,' Dad boomed. 'You're in so much trouble already.'

'I'm not lying!'

Dad let out a moan. 'I'm warning you,' he hissed.

I'd had enough of this. If Dad wasn't prepared to listen, if he insisted on calling me a liar, why should I bother? He knew we were alive, that was the main thing. 'Look,' I said crossly, 'Granny Joss and me and Tag are fine and we'll be in Stockholm in a few hours, ready for the Nobel Prize ceremony at twelve. That's all you need to know.' And I hung up the phone with a foot-stompingly angry CLICK.

I knew my parents were worried about me, but I was with Granny Joss – I was safe and sound. Apart from being near a lion, but the tranquillizer seemed to be working.

Mum and Dad didn't think we should be trekking across Europe to get to the Nobel Prize ceremony, but they were wrong. We'd already made it this far. Why couldn't they see that we *had* to do this? There were no other options.

'Get the ringmaster,' Granny Joss called, jolting me from my thoughts. Frederick ran off, weaving his way through the throng of performers milling around backstage.

'Is everything all right, Granny?' I called. Through the cage bars, I checked for any sign that the lion was waking up. So far, just heavy breathing.

'Everything's fine, love,' Granny Joss replied. 'Just stay that side of the cage, please.'

After a few minutes, the ringmaster hurried towards us, his top hat askew on his head. Rulenska, Kosovo and her brutish henchman followed directly behind. The ringmaster stepped into the cage and knelt down next to the lion, his red coat tails fluttering behind him. 'What happened?' he asked Granny Joss, concerned.

'I believe this lion has been poisoned,' she replied.

A loud GASP went up from the crowd gathered to see what was going on. Rulenska hovered beside me. 'Oh, my,' she muttered.

'You're sure?' the ringmaster asked.

Granny Joss nodded. 'Recently, by the looks of it. It has made him very groggy and sleepy and I would suggest you give him charcoal. It'll bind to the poison and stop it being further absorbed in his blood. Then the poor thing may even need a course of antibiotics before he can move again.'

The ringmaster patted Granny Joss's hand gratefully and stood up. He stepped out of the cage and adjusted his top hat. 'NOBODY MOVE!' he yelled. Everyone froze at the sound of his voice. 'WHOEVER DID THIS TO MY LION COULD STILL BE HERE!'

No one said anything. The wind whistled through the trees in the silence.

I stuck up my hand. 'Um, could *we* go, please?' I called. 'We've got to get to Sweden by morning.'

The ringmaster shook his head. 'Certainly not,' he said. '*No one* moves.'

I caught Granny Joss's eye and we looked at each other in panic. This was what could be described as an 'unexpected escapade'.

'But we're nothing to do with this!' I protested.

The ringmaster looked around the crowd, before his eyes fell on Rulenska, standing beside me. He tapped his chin thoughtfully. 'I wouldn't be so sure of that,' he said mysteriously.

22

CUSTARD PIES AT DAWN!

Everyone silently looked each other up and down. I could feel Rulenska bristle next to me. Behind her, I heard a soft CLICK. From the corner of my eye, I saw Rulenska's bodyguard reach for his gun and square up to the ringmaster.

The circus strongman cracked his knuckles in anticipation.

The clowns all readied their plastic flowers that squirted water.

The elephant prepared to snort peanuts over everyone's head.

And then—

From nowhere, a custard pie flew in a perfect curve across the field, landing with a SPLAT! at Rulenska's feet. She arched an eyebrow. Kosovo the cat splayed his claws, emitted a loud 'HISSSSSSSSS!' and launched himself at the nearest enemy.

The nearest enemy happened to be a man on stilts. As Kosovo leaped up at him, the man stumbled backwards, knocking into a fire-breathing woman, who exhaled a jet of flame in surprise.

The jet of flame was blown into the path of three jugglers, who happened to be practising their juggling skills. And it just so happened that these jugglers were specialists in juggling swords. Sharp, pointy, cutty swords.

Everyone scrambled out of the way as twelve swords were thrown into the air. Clowns bashed into trapeze artists. The strongman bashed into the elephant, and was soon submerged under a heap of snorted-out peanuts. A fortune-teller in a floaty red dress and headscarf smacked into the back of me with a heavy thud, her crystal ball falling to the ground as it collided with my rucksack. I heard the sound of breaking glass as the ball shattered into pieces. I guess she hadn't seen that coming.

Rulenska's henchman grabbed her by the arm and escorted her through the madness, dodging flying sticks of candyfloss and weaving between unicyclists. 'Wait!' I called, but Rulenska didn't hear me. 'Wait for us!'

Frederick the clown appeared next to us and grabbed Granny Joss's arm. 'I can help you escape,' he hissed. 'This way.'

'But Rulenska said she'd have us driven to Sweden,' I said, desperately searching for her in the crowd.

'I can get you to the train station,' Frederick declared. 'You can get to Denmark from there.'

Granny Joss coughed politely. 'We don't have any money,' she said. 'Or passports.'

Frederick thought for a moment. 'When you're on the train,' he said, 'ask for the conductor called Hans. Tell him that I, Frederick, sent you. He'll see you safely to Denmark and give you enough money to go on to Sweden.'

I narrowed my eyes at the clown. This all sounded too good to be true. 'Why are you doing this?'

Frederick shrugged. 'You helped with the lion. It's the least I can do. Rulenska's gone – you've no other choice. Now, come on.' He guided us across the field and out of the circus, his big clown shoes squeaking with every step.

'Here,' Frederick hissed as we approached a small yellow clown car I recognized from the show. He opened up the back door for us. Inside, six clowns cowered, hiding from the fighting.

'Um,' I hesitated. We couldn't *all* fit in there.

'Get in,' Frederick insisted, shoving us both inside.

Granny Joss and I, with Tag on my lap, squished up next to the six clowns in the back. My rucksack dug into my shoulders. I soon wasn't able to feel my legs; one of the clowns was lying on top of them. I felt like the contortionist, all bent over like this.

Frederick climbed into the driver's seat and started pedalling. Pedalling! The clown car inched slowly forward.

I didn't know how far away the station was, when the next train to Denmark would leave, or how long it would take to get there, but I knew we'd better get a wriggle on. 'Can you pedal harder, please?' I called. My voice was all muffled, what with being so squashed.

'Absolutely,' Frederick replied, breaking into a sweat as his feet worked overtime. 'Like I said, helping you is the least I could do. You saved our lion.' He looked at me in the rear-view mirror. 'But,' he added, keeping his voice oh so light and casual, 'I just need to ask a small favour in return.'

I gulped. I *knew* this was too good to be true! And I didn't like the sound of this 'small favour' of his. I didn't like the sound of it at all.

23
ALL ABOARD!

The clown car, with six clowns, Granny Joss, Tag and I squashed inside, crawled along the deserted Hamburg roads at a sickening pace. There were no streetlamps, only the moon to light our way. 'How much longer?' I called.

Frederick, exhausted from pedalling, pointed to something in the distance. 'Almost there!' he replied. 'Not far now.'

Granny Joss sat perfectly still, her eyes fixed straight ahead. I admired her inner strength – her ability to remain calm, no matter what sort of madness unfolded around her. If anything, the last twenty hours or so had shown me that there were *many* things to admire about Granny Joss.

After a few minutes, Frederick let out a cry of relief. 'We're here!' he called, bringing the car to a stop. 'Everybody out.'

Easier said than done. The six clowns unfolded themselves and clambered over us. With a groan, I gripped onto the door handle and heaved myself out after them. I reached back in to help Granny Joss. The two of us stretched by the roadside, making circles with our ankles.

Frederick opened the boot of the car. Another clown clambered out from inside. 'What?' the clown shrugged, like he did this sort of thing all the time.

From the boot, Frederick took out a small wheelie suitcase. He unzipped it slightly, so I could peer inside. 'Hairdryers?' I asked, eyeing a couple near the top. 'Packs of scissors and false nails?'

'Presents,' Frederick replied. 'For my family. They're beauticians,' he added, as if that explained everything. 'It's why it's slightly heavy, I'm afraid. But this is the small favour I need.'

Granny Joss and I exchanged a look. 'What do you want us to do with it?' I asked suspiciously.

'Nothing much,' Frederick replied, all sweetness and light. 'Just look after it on the train.'

'Who do we give it to at the other end?'

Frederick waved his hand away, as if this were a trifling question. 'Oh, don't worry about that,' he said mysteriously. 'It'll sort itself out. Now, come on – I can hear the train.' Frederick grabbed the case and lugged it up the stairs into the station, Granny Joss and I hurrying behind.

The train station was tiny, with a short wooden platform and one single train track. There was no member of staff or ticket machine. But coming round the corner at that very moment was a train with 'COPENHAGEN' written on the front of it.

'That's the one,' Frederick cried, hitting the button on the train doors as it pulled into the station. He lifted the suitcase, Granny Joss and me onto the train in turn. 'Thanks,' he called, waving through the closing door. 'Remember, ask for Hans! And don't let that suitcase out of your sight! And good luck!'

'Good luck?' I called, looking from Frederick to the suitcase and back again. 'What do we need luck for?'

But the train was pulling out of the station and Frederick and the seven clowns soon faded from view. Granny Joss placed a comforting hand on my arm. 'Come on, love. Let's have a sit-down.'

She wheeled the suitcase to four seats by the window. The carriage was almost empty, save for a pale lady with black cropped hair and a tattoo of a dragon snaking up her arm, tapping away on her laptop at the back.

We sank down into the seats. Tag, sensing a change of scene – and a calmer one at that – whimpered to come out. I unbuttoned my coat and let him curl up on the floor by my feet. Bound for Denmark, so close to our goal, I allowed myself to relax. It had been *such* a long day.

'We'll be a couple of hours on here,' Granny Joss said, taking in my obvious fatigue. 'I suggest we get some rest.'

I didn't need to be told twice. The last time I'd slept, I'd been in the back of a car, a gun pointed at me, heading towards certain death. This journey, knowing that we'd soon be in Denmark, which was just a hop, skip and a jump away from Sweden, and that we'd be looked after by Hans the ticket man, was so much more *relaxing*.

Granny Joss and I were asleep within seconds, soothed and comforted by the gentle rhythm of the speeding train as it hurtled through the night. Onwards, onwards, till morning.

24

DO YOU THINK WE'RE EATING SNAILS?

If the 5 trillion spiders in the Netherlands took to eating humans rather than insects, they'd consume all 16.7 million Dutch people in just three days. True story.

(Better not tell my parents that.)

As Granny Joss and I slept soundly, Mum and Dad drove through Holland. Upon disembarking at Calais, they'd hired a vehicle, Mum hesitantly conversing in French with the help of a guidebook. Unfortunately, the guidebook didn't have the phrase

May we hire a four-door saloon? and the rental company only had one vehicle left, so my car-proud dad found himself trundling through France, Germany and now the Netherlands behind the wheel of a minivan completely covered in brown carpet – like fur – with two huge brown ears dangling from either side and a pink tongue swinging from the licence plate. If Dad was already extraceedingly angry with *me* for disobeying him, having to drive Calais's one and only 'comedy rental car' had tipped him over the edge.

My parents soon found themselves in Utrecht, a pretty city in Holland with narrow streets and sleepy canals threading through it. Tall merchant houses lined the canal, most of which had been turned into restaurants, with fairy lights strung up outside and glass doors opening onto the street – all still doing a roaring trade, even at this late hour.

Dad's stomach rumbled. They'd been driving for hours. Mum had nodded off beside him, even though she was meant to be map-reading. The ham sandwiches they'd packed had been demolished ages ago. (Dad didn't care about getting crumbs in *this* car.) On a whim, which was most out of character, Dad pulled up at the side of the road and cut the engine. He gently shook Mum awake. 'I thought we could grab a quick bite,' Dad said. 'Stretch our legs and then carry on.'

I might have mentioned this, but my parents didn't like trying different things. They preferred everything in a set pattern. Mondays, Wednesdays and Fridays were toad in the hole; Tuesdays and Thursdays, omelette and potatoes; Saturday: shepherd's pie; Sunday: roast chicken with all the trimmings. It had been like that forever.

Today's ham sandwiches were most irregular. And now, as a jolly waiter showed Mum and Dad to a candlelit table in the corner of the restaurant, with a most pleasant view of the tree-lined canal, panic set in as they perused the menu. Words like *bitterballen* and *groentesoep met balletjes* swum before their eyes. They had no idea what *stamppot* or *rookworst* meant. Oh, how they wished there were pictures.

'Maybe they'll do us cheese on toast?' Mum whispered, trying to make the best of it. She smiled broadly at Dad. It had been ages since they'd gone out for dinner, just the two of them. In this quiet, pretty, *romantic* setting, she had to admit, it was all rather nice.

Pointing at words they didn't understand, together Mum and Dad ordered some sort of meat dish with potatoes and vegetables. They were both starving. There was nothing else to eat. '*Bon appetit,*' Mum said, hesitantly tucking into something grey and fleshy on her plate. She chewed slowly for a moment and then— 'Mmm,' she said, swallowing with relish. 'That's really rather pleasant.'

Dad followed suit. 'It tastes like sausage,' he said, allowing the food to roll around his mouth. 'I think it'll do the trick.'

Spontaneously, Mum reached across the table for Dad's hand and squeezed it. 'I'm so angry with Matilda, but I just want her to come home,' she said. 'She will be all right, won't she?'

Dad put down his knife and fork and held Mum's hand in his. 'She's resourceful,' he replied. 'She's inventive. And she doesn't take no for an answer.'

Tears welled up in Mum's eyes. 'She's really rather special, isn't she?'

Dad laughed. 'It's hard to believe she's ours at times.'

They sat like that for a little while, holding each other's hand, enjoying each other's company. The Dutch delicacies were going down a treat. They even ordered dessert – *flensjes met roomijs:* little Dutch pancakes with ice cream.

And as they walked back to the car, dodging out of the way as students whizzed past on bicycles, they felt young again. Dad forgot about being stressed at work. Mum forgot about the book she *had* to read for Monday's book club. They knew they were on a mission to get to me and Granny Joss and that this had been a mere pit stop; a chance to refuel. But it felt as if they were on holiday – trying new things, getting out of the routine of the daily grind.

Mum and Dad got back into the car and set off on the road towards Stockholm renewed and reinvigorated. It was, if they were being honest, *exactly* what they'd both needed.

They could thank me later.

25

RULENSKA'S
DIAMONDS

408 miles to Stockholm

I slept soundly for most of our train journey, though my dreams were interspersed with custard pies, out-of-control hot-air balloons and a hissing white cat with piercing amber eyes.

I awoke after we'd crossed the border from Germany into Denmark, hurtling towards Copenhagen. I couldn't help but marvel as we whizzed through each station – crossing the sea at Puttgarden, on through Lolland, Vordinborg, Tappernøje. I'd never heard of such strange-yet-magical-sounding places.

I stretched my aching legs in front of me and checked my watch. 5.08 a.m. – 6.08 a.m. in Denmark. We'd been on the train for hours. Granny Joss gazed out of the window at the muddy brown fields and countryside we were racing past, Tag curled up neatly in her lap. We were still the only ones in the carriage, apart from The Girl With the Dragon Tattoo at the back.

'It's been quite the adventure,' Granny Joss said wistfully, looking back at me with tears in her eyes. 'And I wouldn't have wanted to share it with anyone else. Morning, love.'

I smiled sadly at her, suddenly feeling guilty McGuilty. 'I'm sorry, Granny,' I said, my voice small, 'that I didn't find out more about your life until now.' All those visits when I'd leave Mum and Dad with Granny Joss while I spent my time with Grandad Wilf, inventing things. Because no one ever spoke of it, I'd never even *bothered* to find out what Granny Joss did before she'd had Dad. My face flushed with the shame of that.

I thought back to Granny Joss expertly landing the hot-air balloon on top of the Eiffel Tower. Of her stepping into the cage of the lion she'd shot with a tranquillizer dart. She was, quite simply, FIERCE. 'Or about how brilliant you are,' I added.

Granny Joss squeezed my hand. 'I couldn't have got this far without you,' she smiled. '*You* did this, my love. You. I'm so proud of you.'

I let out a deep sigh. 'It's just a shame Mum and Dad can't be here as well.' I looked out of the window at the countryside whizzing past. 'I'm sure they would have liked this. Though I know they don't like trying new stuff.'

Granny Joss sensed my mood had shifted. 'Matilda?' she asked gently in her soft Scottish lilt.

'I don't think Mum and Dad get me,' I explained, feeling hot pricks behind my eyes. 'They like me being obsessed with science and inventing and everything, but I think they think I'm a bit weird.' I twirled a strand of hair round my finger.

Granny Joss fiddled with the sleeve of her white-knitted jumper. She took a few moments before answering. 'That's my fault,' she said quietly.

'What?'

'You're not weird, dearie,' Granny Joss stressed. 'You're *bold*. And it's the ones who are bold and take chances in this life who make history, let me tell you.' She looked skywards, as if searching for the right words. 'It's my fault your dad is – well, the way he is.' She spotted my confusion. 'After I left the Observatory,' she continued, 'I took a variety of positions at different scientific institutions, trying to move on. Trying to do good work, despite how I'd been treated.' She shifted in her seat uncomfortably. 'Before your dad was your age, we'd moved eight times. It was hard for him to settle or make friends, because he never knew how long we'd be staying. I think, if I'm being honest, that's why he likes routine now. He likes to organize, to plan. Because of me.'

I stared at Granny Joss, open-mouthed. Dad had never mentioned anything about his childhood before. As her words sank in, I could feel the fire in my belly recede a little. So maybe *that's* why Dad didn't like taking risks or doing anything out of the ordinary – because he'd had so much uncertainty when he was younger.

I stared out the window as I thought about the adventure we'd had in the last twenty-four hours. In truth, it was the *only* adventure I'd ever had with Granny Joss, what with me having preferred to spend all my time with Grandad Wilf. And, though I didn't say anything, I knew full well that, at eighty years old, this was likely to be Granny Joss's *last* big adventure.

Granny Joss gave a big sniff at that point. Not just to wipe the tears from her eyes, because she crooked her head to her armpit and inhaled. 'Hmm,' she muttered. 'Not as fragrant as I would have liked.'

I gave myself a big sniff too. She was right. All the running, flying, sweating, hugging and snuggling Tag had taken its toll – my clothes had a musty mud/ sweat/dirty-animal smell to them.

Before I could do anything about it, the train screeched to a sudden halt. Tag's eyes flew open and darted around the carriage. I gripped hold of his lead tightly so he couldn't scamper off.

The sound of footsteps pounded down the train corridor, followed by a series of shouts. I didn't understand what was going on, for the cries were in German, and I understood that even less than French.

The door to the carriage opened and two train conductors barged in. One was as wide as he was tall; the other was slim and pale, with short blond hair. Both were wearing grey jackets with gold buttons on. '*FAHRKARTEN!*' he shouted at us. '*FAHRKARTEN!*'

'Um, Hans?' I asked, remembering the name the clown had given us. 'Is one of you Hans? Frederick said to ask for you.'

The men ignored me and marched up to Granny Joss. '*PASS!*' they demanded.

The girl with the dragon tattoo stood up. 'He wants your tickets and passports,' she called in broken English from the other end of the carriage.

'We don't have any,' I replied, panic setting in. 'There was a clown called Frederick at the circus in Hamburg. He put us on this train and said to ask for Hans. Can you tell them that?'

The girl with the dragon tattoo couldn't help showing her surprise, but relayed it to the train conductors nonetheless. They looked Granny Joss and me up and down. And then they spotted Tag.

The short train conductor turned bright pink. 'Animals are not allowed on here,' the girl with the dragon tattoo repeated, translating his words. 'If you can't show your tickets and passports, you'll be thrown off. Sorry.' The girl smiled apologetically. 'That "sorry" was me, by the way, not him.'

Granny Joss and I looked at each other. Had Frederick lied? Where was this Hans he'd told us to ask for? Had we been well and truly stitched up by a clown?

The two train conductors herded us towards the train doors, so with no other choice I grabbed the wheelie suitcase, clutched Tag's lead in one hand, my rucksack in the other and clambered off the train. I turned to help Granny Joss down after me.

We were in the middle of nowhere. Just a single railway track with muddy brown fields all around us. 'Fat lot of good you were,' I shouted at the conductors as the doors closed on us. They hadn't even *tried* to find out where Hans was.

I gulped. As the train pulled away and sped off down the track, it dawned on me that there *was* no Hans. Frederick had made the whole thing up, just to get us out of the circus and on the train to Denmark. But why?

My question was answered that very moment. For with no word of warning, the wheelie suitcase began to move.

'What the—?' Granny Joss exclaimed, backing away in surprise.

The zip of the suitcase slowly came undone with a loud *zzzeeeaarrrcccpppp*. Tag barked at it in fright.

From out of the suitcase appeared a leg. Another leg. Then two arms, a torso and a head. Granny Joss and I gasped in surprise as the contortionist, still in her bejewelled leotard from the show, burst from the suitcase, scattering packets of false eyelashes and bottles of nail glue on the ground. 'Ooof,' she muttered as she stretched and flexed her limbs. 'Yeeeoow.'

I couldn't help myself and burst into applause before I knew what I was doing. The contortionist bowed, her dazzling leotard sparkling in the morning light.

'What's going on?' Granny Joss asked, looking from the contortionist to the suitcase and back again. 'Frederick said it was presents for his family in there.'

The contortionist gave us another twirl. I shielded my eyes from her costume. I'd never seen so many stones on one before. I peered closer at the pink leotard, every inch of it covered in jewels. 'Hang on a second,' I said, working it all out. 'You've got more stones on it than last night.' I clasped my hand to my mouth in shock. 'Rulenska's missing diamonds!'

Beside me, Granny Joss gasped in shock too. 'You're a jewel thief!' she cried.

The contortionist crossed her arms in protest. (Round the back of her head, for she wanted to show off.) 'Now look here,' she said in a thick German accent. 'The ringmaster owed us a lot of money, but he never pays us. I knew he was planning on – how do you say it – crossing Rulenska? Using a friend of 'is. Doctor Françoise Bertrand. So as soon as the ringmaster had stolen the diamonds from Rulenska, Frederick and I stole the diamonds from *him*. We plotted to smuggle them out of Germany somewhere no one would ever look.'

'A suitcase,' I whispered.

'My *leotard*,' the contortionist corrected.

Granny Joss thought for a moment. 'So the poisoned lion was a distraction?' she asked. 'And it *wasn't* Rulenska?'

The contortionist nodded. 'We gave Samson just enough of a herbal potion to cause a scene,' she said.

'We didn't want to hurt him, and certainly not kill him. We're not monsters.'

'Just jewel thieves,' I said simply.

The contortionist shrugged. 'Whatever.'

'But what about us?' Granny Joss asked. 'How do we get to Sweden now?'

A small flash of sorrow flickered across the contortionist's face. She'd spent the past few hours curled up in the suitcase, listening to our plan. 'I'm sorry,' she said, sounding genuinely apologetic. 'I couldn't have done this without you. We needed someone to take the suitcase on the train without arousing suspicion. But I simply can't help, I'm afraid.' And with that, the contortionist bent over into a crab and scuttled off down the road. Now she really *was* showing off.

'What about all this – *stuff*?' I called after her, eyeing the suitcase's contents on the ground.

'Keep it!' the contortionist called over her shoulder. 'It was only for show, in case anyone looked inside.' And, just like that, she was gone.

Not knowing what else to do, I slumped down on the ground. I didn't even care that it was muddy.

'Come on, love,' Granny Joss soothed. 'Chin up. What is it you always say? Thomas Edison failed a thousand times?'

I let out a puff of air. 'We're criminals, Granny,' I said crossly. 'We've unwittingly smuggled stolen diamonds out of the country. We're in Denmark without tickets or passports. We're four hundred miles from the Nobel Prize ceremony with only five hours to go. There's no way you can walk there. There's no sign of a taxi. We've come so far from Arnos Yarm – we're only one country away now, instead of four. But we've still not made it.' A sudden thought popped into my head. 'Oh no,' I said, panic rising within me. 'Oh, please no.' I quickly took off my rucksack and unfastened the zip. That tinkling noise I'd heard earlier, when the fortune-teller had bashed into me at the circus. That faint tinkling noise that sounded like glass smashing – I thought it had only been her crystal ball, but what if—

'Careful!' Granny Joss called, for she'd spotted what had happened. 'You'll cut yourself. Here, let me.'

Granny Joss gingerly rummaged inside my rucksack and after a moment pulled out three big shards of glass. The photographic plate had smashed into pieces.

'The proof,' I whispered.

We'd come all this way. We'd tackled so many hurdles and yet here we were, the rectangular glass plate of Granny Joss's planet smashed to smithereens. 'I didn't think to pack glue,' I muttered. 'We can't put it back together again.' This whole thing had been a complete waste of time. 'I've failed, Granny. I've let you down.' I pulled my knees up to my chin and let out a huge wail. All the worry and stress of the past twenty-four hours worked itself out of my body in the form of huge, wracking sobs.

Granny Joss winced as she sat down on the hard ground next to me. 'Shh,' she soothed, stroking my hair. 'What nonsense. I've had a terrific adventure. And we're not stopping yet. Think of Thomas Edison! Think of Marie Curie! Would *they* have given up?'

A huge sob caught in my throat. My eyes were puffy with tears. I could have done with one of Mum's lavender-scented tissues. 'What's to say that if – *if*,' I stressed, 'we even get to Sweden, the Nobel Prize committee people will listen to us? I couldn't make

Mr Yonker or Mr Dorfman or Mr Varney or Mr Keegan my headteacher or Mum or Dad or *anyone* listen to me about Thomas Thomas and the stupid Grand Science Prize. I've broken the only proof we had. This is the end, Granny. Grandad's stupid saying was wrong. Because, guess what? It's not all right, Granny. It's extraceedingly *not* all right.'

Drained of energy and drive, feeling like a total failure, I put my head down onto my knees and sobbed and sobbed and sobbed.

26

THIS HOTEL HAS NO TOOTHPASTE

Professor Tarquin Smocks had never been to Sweden before. He'd had a bit of a shock when he'd left the airport late on Saturday afternoon and been greeted by the grey Scandinavian climate. He was closely followed by a stoop-shouldered bald man in his sixties, who looked as if he was carrying the weight of the world with him. (He wasn't, but he *was* carrying the three suitcases, two suit bags, a make-up case and the hat box that Professor Smocks had insisted on bringing.) 'Keep up, Trevor,' Professor Smocks barked as he bustled to the taxi rank. 'We haven't got all day.'

Trevor Foot had dedicated the last fifty years of his life to working for Professor Smocks, but he'd never got used to his boss's sharp temper and rude demands.

He let out a sigh as he scurried after Professor Smocks through the crowd of tourists towards the line of taxis. He was too stressed to see that he'd trodden on a man's toes. He was too laden with baggage to realize that he'd accidentally barged into a woman's suitcase, springing open the lock and exposing her underwear to all and sundry.

As Trevor Foot bundled everything into the boot of the first taxi in the queue, he slid into the back seat alongside Professor Smocks and retrieved a guidebook from his pocket. One of the perks of working for Professor Smocks for so long had meant that he'd seen the world, for Professor Smocks travelled here, there and everywhere, giving speeches and talks at conferences and events around the world. Trevor Foot had kept a diary for the last fifty years, bulging with details of every single trip they'd been on. He very often re-read it, remembering the day in Thailand when he'd swum with turtles while Professor Smocks had given an after-lunch speech at the university, or the time they'd been invited to dine with the Sultan of Brunei after Professor Smocks had been a guest on a chat show in the Middle East.

Trevor had never been to Sweden before either and was looking forward to exploring its magnificent sights. 'I thought we could take a stroll around Drottningholm Palace after dinner,' he said, flicking through the guidebook. 'It's a late-sixteenth-century castle. Then we could journey to the *Gamla Stan*, Stockholm's historic old town.' He didn't catch the look of annoyance on Professor Smocks's face. 'And I wouldn't mind,' Trevor added shyly, 'visiting the ABBA museum. I must confess to being a fan of their music.'

Professor Smocks scoffed. 'I hardly think so.'

'Oh well, I don't mind going on my own,' Trevor said hastily. 'I completely understand if you don't want—'

'It's not that,' Professor Smocks replied, waving his hand as if batting away Trevor's concerns. 'You may go if there's time. But I'll need you to get everything ready for tomorrow.'

Trevor frowned. 'Everything *is* ready, sir,' he replied.

Professor Smocks gazed out of the window, taking in the bustling streets of Stockholm. 'I've been waiting over fifty years for this moment, Trevor,' he sighed. 'I need to look my best.'

'You will, sir, you will.'

'I'll need my suit double-pressed,' Professor Smocks ploughed on. 'And steamed. I'll need my cravat triple-ironed, so it gets out all those annoying little creases. And make sure my shoes are buffed and shined. With the Raven boot polish. None of that cheap muck you used last time.'

'All right, but—' Trevor stuttered.

'I'd like vanilla-scented candles in my room,' Professor Smocks continued. 'They help me relax. As will a massage. And a mudpack on my face. I want my feet pumiced and my toenails clipped, and my ears and nose hair trimmed. And I'll only trust *you* to do it.'

Trevor's face fell. It dawned on him that not only would he *not* be seeing the sights of Stockholm as he originally thought, but that he'd be spending the evening in close proximity to Professor Smocks's toenails.

As the taxi drew to a stop, he packed away his guidebook with a heavy heart and helped Professor Smocks out of the car.

They were booked into the nearest hotel to Stockholm's City Hall. The hotel had never been so busy, for everyone who was due to receive an award, and everyone who had travelled from various countries to attend the ceremony, had checked in.

So while Trevor Foot did all his ironing chores, Professor Smocks hobnobbed with some important people over dinner, posed for photos and took a stroll through the centre of Stockholm, marvelling at its colourful wooden buildings on the river front. He even nipped into the ABBA museum, enjoying it immensely.

After his massage, he had his best night's sleep in ages.

This morning, as Professor Smocks sat on the end of the bed while Trevor filed his nails and combed his hair, he rehearsed his winner's speech over and over again. He'd be sure to thank his parents, and lament the fact they were no longer here to witness his greatest moment. He'd thank his colleagues at the Royal Observatory in Greenwich too. It would make him appear humble, while also letting the world know how much *better* than them he was.

A shadow crossed Professor Smocks's face at that thought. He wouldn't thank *all* of his colleagues, obviously. No point bringing up Jocelyn Moore's name. He shuddered as he remembered that nasty business fifty years ago; no – the less said about that, the better.

It was the one thing that had haunted him all these years. Not what he had done – because in science and progress, sacrifices *had* to be made; the creator of the Nobel Prizes, Alfred Nobel himself, had known great personal loss— No, the one thing that bugged Professor Smocks was if someday, somehow, the *truth* should ever be found out.

Professor Smocks suppressed that thought. He'd kept tabs on Jocelyn Moore over the years, following her movement from scientific institution to scientific institution. But all that had stopped fifteen years ago – he hadn't heard anything of her since. She was probably off living a quiet life somewhere. There was nothing to say she was even still alive.

As Trevor plucked a few stray eyebrow hairs from his face, Professor Smocks smiled. Jocelyn Moore was a failure. He, Tarquin Neville Ignatius, was a winner. The Nobel Prize was his! And nothing and no one was going to stop him from getting that award.

27

ONE GOOD TURN
DESERVES ANOTHER

Isn't it strange what pops into your head when you need it to? Maybe it had been Granny Joss's words. Maybe it had been the chemical elements on my purple periodic table T-shirt reminding me.

My face was raw from crying. My stomach growled, for it had been hours since Rulenska's meal. I felt crushed under the weight of my tiredness.

'Think of Thomas Edison,' Granny Joss had said, trying to comfort me. 'And Marie Curie.'

And so, from nowhere, this rattled around my brain:

Life is not easy for any of us. But what of that? We must have perseverance and confidence in ourselves. The first principle: Never to let oneself be beaten down by persons or events.

I'd read that in a book about Marie Curie. She discovered not one but two chemical elements — polonium and radium — in a time when there were hardly any female scientists, and she was the first woman ever to win a Nobel Prize. She became the first *person* ever to win two.

And you don't win two Nobel Prizes by letting yourself be beaten down by people or events.

I leaped to my feet. 'Right, Granny,' I said, holding out my hand to her. 'New plan. We're going to walk along the railway track until we get to the next station. We're going to wait for the train and force ourselves on. And we're going to get to Sweden, by hook or by crook.'

Granny Joss looked up at me, her blue eyes twinkling in delight. 'That's my girl,' she smiled, grabbing hold of my hand and getting to her feet.

'But first, we're going to fix this!' I carefully took the fragments of photographic plate from inside my rucksack. An idea had whizz-popped into my head, you see. We'd need to put the plate back together and, all right, we didn't have any *proper* glue for glass. But what did we have? SCIENCE! And false nails!

I'd spotted a little bottle of nail glue on the ground by the contortionist's suitcase and grabbed it. If it was gluey enough to stick nails on your fingers, maybe it would be gluey enough for us. 'Cyano-acrylate,' I said slowly, reading the back of the bottle. 'What's that?'

Granny Joss beamed at me. 'It's the solution, you clever sausage,' she replied. 'That's what. It's the compound used in superglue.'

Yesss! Frederick and the contortionist had done us a favour, after all! I squeezed the nail glue from the tube over the edges of the glass and held them while it dried. I worked extraceedingly carefully – we didn't have time for me to go to hospital for stitches if I cut myself. Granny Joss joined in, piecing the shards together like one of her jigsaw puzzles. This was *far* more important than any we'd completed at Canterbury Cares Care Home, though.

'Ta-da!' I said after a few minutes. The photographic plate was wonky and haphazard, but it was now all in one piece. It would be enough to show the Nobel Prize committee.

Granny Joss clapped her hands in delight. 'Oh, well done, Matilda!'

I carefully folded the photographic plate in my jumper and placed it back inside my rucksack, got to my feet, entwined Tag's lead round my hand and led Granny Joss along the railway track. I felt renewed, confident. There was *still* a chance!

We walked in the direction the train had been heading before the plump train conductor had so rudely thrown us off it. The sun was rising in the sky, but it was still a bitter cold December morning. 'You know something, Matilda?' Granny Joss said, placing her hand on my arm as we walked. 'You astound me.'

My eyebrows shot up in surprise.

'I mean it,' Granny Joss laughed. 'Even when all seems lost, you've brushed yourself off and are trying again. You never give up. That's remarkable.' She squeezed my arm appreciatively. She didn't have to say anything for me to know how important it was to carry on. 'You take after your grandad,' she added. 'Not just for your love of inventing, but for your – belief.' She looked up to the sky and I thought I could see tears in her eyes. 'All these years, your grandad kept my paperwork, and that glass plate. Even when I no longer believed in myself, your grandad did. Just like you do. I'll never be able to thank you both enough.' She leaned over and gave me a peck on the cheek.

Before I could say anything, Tag shot off across the field, the dog lead flying out of my hand. 'Woah!' I called. 'Tag! Come back!'

The crazy dog raced through the overgrown grass, away from the railway track, his little legs working overtime as he sprinted off into the distance. That was all we needed.

'Tag!' Granny Joss called. 'He's going the wrong way.'

I didn't know whether to go after him. What if a train came at any moment?

Suddenly Tag stopped running and stood perfectly still, ears pricked and alert. And then he started yapping, as if calling to us, looking off in the distance and then back at us again.

This all seemed rather familiar – like the time Tag had called us over to Svetlanka and Chris P's boat. Maybe he was trying to do the same. I frowned. Not that there were any boats in the middle of the countryside.

But still. It was thanks to Tag that we'd even made it to Calais.

'This way,' I said, clutching Granny Joss's hand and striding off towards the dog, who was still yapping at the wind.

Just as we approached, the strangest thing happened. In the distance came a low humming sound. BRRRRRUUUUUMMMM!

'What's that?' I asked, looking all about us. There was nothing but empty brown fields.

Granny Joss cocked an ear to one side. 'No idea,' she said after a moment.

BRRRRUUUUUMMMMM!! The ground vibrated as the sound got nearer. As we approached Tag, he stopped yapping and pawed at my legs, pleased to see me again.

'What's all this about, boy?' I asked, reaching down and stroking his ears.

BRRRRRRUUUUMMMM!!! There it was again. It sounded like the rumble of thunder. It sounded like a million washing machines about to take off.

A motorbike. Several motorbikes.

Like a volcanic eruption of beards, metal and leather trousers, a convoy of Hell's Angels sped on shiny black motorbikes towards us. 'Watch out!' I cried, pulling Granny Joss to one side. I clasped my hands to my ears. The noise was deafening.

'Oi oi!' a voice called from among the stream of bikes. I shielded my eyes from the morning sun and peered into the throng of bikers. Most of whom were gruff-looking men. They weren't the sort of people I'd want to be caught with on a dark night. They weren't the sort of people I wanted to be caught with RIGHT NOW in *broad daylight*.

'All right, my lovers?' the voice called in a broad Bristolian accent. 'Stockholm, wasn't it?'

That's when I saw him. 'Mickey?' I yelled in surprise. Channel-swimming Mickey! On the back of a motorbike, arms clasped round the waist of a burly, bearded biker. 'What are you doing here?' I cried. It seemed *so* long since we were all sipping tea and eating biscuits together. Seeing him again comforted me enormously. I flung my arms round him in joy.

'Steady on,' Mickey grumbled as I latched onto his waist. He smiled in spite of himself. 'One good turn deserves another,' he said amiably. 'I finally swam all the way to Calais and thought I'd make a day of it. I met Davos, here' – Mickey indicated the man on the bike whose torso he clutched – 'while I was out on the town and he invited me to join a little road trip to Sweden. I remembered you were on your way there, and I was so inspired by your mission, I thought, Why not? You only live once. We happened to be passing along when I heard a dog yapping. I asked Davos to make a slight detour in case it was in pain. And then I saw your granny's hair in the distance. And here you are!' He looked down at me. 'So come on, then.'

My jaw nearly hit the ground. Our prayers had been answered! I checked my watch. 6.48 a.m. 'It's seven forty-eight,' I said to Mickey, remembering to add an hour on. 'Do you think we can get to Stockholm for twelve?'

Mickey frowned. 'It'll be tricky,' he stated. 'But when has that ever stopped you?'

I hoisted my rucksack onto my back and helped Granny Joss into a sidecar attached to one of the motorbikes. There was no time to lose! I scooped Tag up and plonked him inside another sidecar, pecking him on the top of his head as I fastened a helmet onto him. 'Thanks, Tag,' I whispered, for he'd been the one to alert Mickey to us.

Finally, I climbed inside my own sidecar. It was attached to the motorbike of a lady with a shaved head and a skull-and-crossbones leather waistcoat. 'Hello,' the woman said in a surprisingly soft and gentle voice. 'I'm Gertrude.'

I fastened my helmet tightly under my chin. 'Matilda,' I replied, mustering a smile. I was overwhelmed by this big gang of bikers taking us all the way to Sweden, to be honest.

Gertrude nodded. 'I know,' she said. 'Mickey's been telling us all about you.'

I truly couldn't believe it. Just when the chips were down, just when I thought we'd failed, along comes Mickey to the rescue. And he *wouldn't* have done had Granny Joss and I not helped him in the first place, for he wouldn't have wanted to come to Sweden or recognized Granny Joss and her frizzy white hair. Funny how things work out.

And maybe, just maybe, everything *would* be all right in the end.

28

TO SWEDEN! TILL VALHALL!

Mickey and his team of Hell's Angels zoomed along the back roads of Denmark to avoid border control. We flew through magical-sounding village after magical-sounding village – Køge, Malmö, Lund – before bombing down the country roads of Skövde, all while Mickey blasted out ABBA's greatest hits on his sound system. 'When in Rome,' Mickey had shouted with glee to me. I was happy to sing along – I loved *Mamma Mia*.

Mariestad now. On through Kumla. I looked over at Tag in the sidecar next to mine. His ears were pinned back under his helmet and his tongue was hanging out, but his tail was wagging like the clappers. He was having a whale of a time.

We sped past a small fishing village in Katrineholm, laughing as a group of weather-beaten fishermen stared open-mouthed at the horde of bikers, with an elderly woman, a little girl and a dog in three of the attached sidecars.

We passed several IKEA outlets, and I made a mental note to tell Dad they were having a sale on Aneboda wardrobes. Perhaps it would be enough to put me back in his good books.

And as Mickey hit 'play' on one of ABBA's most famous hits, the whole convoy of bikers joined in with 'Waterloo'. I changed the lyrics to fit in with our mission:

'My my, at the Nobel Prize ceremony, Professor Smocks did surrender!

Oh yeah, and Granny Joss has met her destiny in quite a brilliant way.

The history books on the shelf, will finally be correeeecccctteedd!!!'

I had to admit – we were having fun. I glanced at my watch. 9.55 a.m. So it was actually 10.55 a.m. We had just over an hour until the ceremony started. Only a few more miles to go. We could do this!

29

LOOK BEHIND YOU!

Unbeknownst to me, Granny Joss, Tag, Mickey, Davos, Gertrude or the rest of the Hell's Angels, it so happened that bombing down the same streets of the village of Flen, directly behind us, in a comedy car that looked like a giant dog, were Mum and Dad.

A funny thing had happened since their restaurant stop in Utrecht. They'd spent the past few hours talking about their feelings – ranging from anger at my disobeying them and running away, then putting funny ideas into Granny Joss's head, to something resembling admiration for us both. Their daughter had trekked across the Continent, just like that! I had made a plan and stuck to it! They *had* to admire my spirit, at the very least.

Since their romantic meal, Mum and Dad had reminisced about the time they'd met each other. Both had been studying at university and they'd gone to a party neither of them had wanted to attend. They'd got chatting about their favourite music and decided to break into the university music room to record a song together. Dad played the drums; Mum covered tambourine and lead vocals, dancing barefoot in the studio booth. They'd had the best time.

Until a security guard reported them and they'd almost been thrown off their courses. Mum's parents were so angry. They warned Dad to stay away, for he was clearly a bad influence. But he'd already fallen in love with Mum and didn't want to. So he changed his ways. He knuckled down, studied and worked hard to prove himself.

He had been the same ever since. Especially when I came along. Dad had wanted me to have a normal, stable childhood; not moving around constantly like he had done. That's why he was so set on routine. That's why he was so set on having a *sensible* life.

But now, as the strains of a familiar song drifted through the air, the very song he and Mum had

249

recorded in the studio that night, he was taken back twenty years.

Mum and Dad both spontaneously broke out into the chorus of 'Waterloo', bellowing out the lyrics, their voices making up for the lack of drum or tambourine as they smiled at each other.

Dad wound the window down and waved his arms in the crisp December air as they bombed along the narrow Swedish roads, the dog ears of the car waggling up and down, the pink tongue over the licence plate swinging back and forth. Dad didn't know how to turn the effects off, but really, there wasn't any harm in being a *little* bit silly and impulsive every now and again, was there? Mum and Dad stuck their heads out of the window and howled at the wind like dogs.

It was, quite simply, the happiest they'd been in years.

30

LOOK BEHIND YOU,
PART TWO!

Unbeknownst to me, Granny Joss, Tag, Mickey, Davos, Gertrude, the Hell's Angels *or* Mum and Dad, it so happened that bombing down the same streets of the village of Flen, directly behind them, was a sleek silver car with a gruff brute in a suit behind the wheel and a Kosovan gangster in the back.

The ringmaster had eventually confessed to stealing Rulenska's diamonds with the help of Doctor Bertrand. Trouble was, he didn't know where they were now. So Rulenska had 'encouraged' every single circus performer to talk, until *someone* had let slip that the diamonds were in a suitcase carried by me and Granny Joss. That someone had been the mime artist. Typical.

As the familiar strains of an ABBA song drifted through the air, tears welled up in Rulenska's eyes. It was the song her mother used to sing to her and her sister when they were little. Rulenska blew into a tissue. She had no idea where her sister currently was. She only knew what I'd told her – that Svetlanka had married a man called Chris P Duck (what a ridiculous name, Rulenska had thought to herself) and was living in England.

Rulenska made a vow as she hummed along to the ABBA track. As soon as this whole being-double-crossed-over-a-bag-of-diamonds business was dealt with, she would make it her mission to find her sister once and for all.

31

LOOK BEHIND— OH, SERIOUSLY, WHEN WILL THIS CONVOY END?

Unbeknownst to me, Granny Joss, Tag, Mickey etc. etc. – you know the drill – it so happened that bombing down the backstreets, yada yada yada, was Chris P Duck and his glamorous blonde wife, Svetlanka. They, like Mickey, had been so inspired by Granny Joss and me that they wanted to see for themselves how it would all end. Instead of returning to England after they'd dropped us off in Calais, they'd spent a rather lovely night in France, before driving on to Sweden.

Chris P saw that Svetlanka was a trifle sad, for she too had heard the strains of an ABBA song blasting out. Chris P knew it was the song she used to sing with her family and he hummed it now with her in solidarity. She smiled at him gratefully, knowing that she really had married a lovely, kind, understanding man.

She still hated his name, though.

32

TO SWEDEN! TILL VALHALL, PART TWO

In one long line, a series of motorbikes, cars and one comedy dog minivan sped through the quiet country roads of Södertälje towards the capital city of Stockholm. The few villagers who found themselves out and about that Sunday morning had to jump out of the way as the parade of vehicles raced past. A tractor heading towards us careered off the road into a field, the driver shaking his fist as we whizzed through.

I checked my watch. 12.17 p.m. Swedish time. We were late. I hoped against hope that Professor Smocks hadn't been given his award yet.

Stockholm City Hall was an historic building situated on the waterfront just off the *Hantverkargatan* main road and overlooking the Royal Palace.

Inside, scientists, writers, philosophers, professors and dignitaries, the British, French, German, Belgian, Danish and Swedish Prime Ministers, news cameras and journalists, and the King and Queen of Sweden all sat in their seats, dressed in their finest gowns and tuxedos, waiting for the ceremony to begin.

On stage, the winners of the Nobel Prizes – Literature, Economics, Chemistry, Peace and Medicine – sat proudly. Smack bang in the middle of the row was Professor Smocks himself, wearing his best purple velvet suit and yellow cravat and grinning around at everyone like a loon.

We were still a few minutes away. The gang of Hell's Angels screeched through the streets of Stockholm, following *Stadhus* signs towards the City Hall. No one spoke Swedish. Technically, we could be heading anywhere.

'There!' Granny Joss yelled, pointing to a bell tower in the next road. The motorbikes zoomed round the corner onto a cobbled pavement, and the City Hall came into view. It was an old brown rectangular building, with white stone pillars marking the front entrance and a totally pointless low iron gate that only came up to my knees surrounding the hall.

As Gertrude cut the engine, I quickly dismounted and took off my helmet. 'Thanks, Gertrude,' I said breathlessly. I squeezed Mickey in gratitude and helped Granny Joss and Tag out of their sidecars, thrusting the dog into the front pocket of my dungarees once more.

I took a deep breath. 'Ready?' I asked excitedly. Granny Joss nodded back at me, slightly stunned, neither of us *quite* believing we'd actually made it. With no time to lose, we raced towards the grand wooden double doors, Mickey following us at a slightly slower pace.

At that moment, a tall security guard stepped in front of us, blocking the entrance. 'Invited guests only,' the man huffed, looking me up and down. I didn't even want to *think* about how untidy my hair was right now.

'What?' I looked at Granny Joss in panic.

'If you don't have an invite, I can't let you in,' the man bleated in broken English. 'Dignitaries only.' I could tell from his face that he didn't think Granny Joss and I were.

My mouth dropped open in shock. I couldn't believe we'd made it here but were unable to go inside because of this stupid man. 'Please,' I said, tears welling up in my eyes. 'We've made it this far.'

The security guard pointed upwards to a police helicopter hovering overhead. 'Tight security. Lots of important people inside,' he barked.

I looked at Granny Joss in *wild* panic. I hadn't even *thought* about security. I'd figured we'd just be able to stroll in. How were we going to get around this?

'I demand you let her in!' a voice boomed behind me at that very moment. A familiar theatrical voice with northern tones. I spun round to see—

'Brian Colin Ramsbottom!' I yelled, surprised.

He bowed deeply. 'At your service. Now, you, sir' – he waggled his finger at the security guard – 'you let this girl and her granny in straightaway!'

Before anyone could say anything, at that moment, we heard the distinct sound of police sirens screeching round the corner. I turned to see three police cars hurtling down the cobbled street towards us.

As they skidded to a halt outside the City Hall, several uniformed policemen clambered out of the cars and surrounded us in a semicircle.

'Stop where you are!' the chief policeman shouted at Brian, Granny Joss and me. The security guard looked us all up and down with renewed interest. He didn't know who we were, but this wasn't half exciting.

All three of us threw our hands in the air. 'Bother it,' Brian Ramsbottom hissed. 'They've tracked me down.'

'What?' I shrieked. 'I thought you said you'd deal with them. That you'd take the flak for the hot-air balloon landing?'

'I sort of ran away too,' Brian muttered. 'The French police must have got on to this lot that I – we – were here.'

Oh, great. As if one security guard not letting us in wasn't a big enough hurdle, we somehow had to escape the Swedish police too. The Exploding Bag Trick would have been *so* handy right now.

Just at that moment, we heard the unmistakable squeal of a glamorous Kosovan woman. 'I demand that you let them in straightaway!'

I looked past Brian to see Svetlanka tottering precariously in heels on the cobbled pavements towards us, Chris P Duck bustling beside her. 'They have been on more of a journey than you can possibly imagine!'

'Oh, for goodness' sake,' the security guard cried. 'I'm just trying to do my job.'

'Svetlanka?' I exclaimed. 'Chris P? What are you doing here?'

Chris P Duck smiled at me, his captain's hat perched jauntily on his head. 'There was no way we weren't going to see how this ended,' he explained. 'All right, Mickey?' he added, spotting him.

Before anyone could say anything, at that moment, another loud shriek rang out. 'My sister!' I looked past Chris P and Svetlanka to see Rulenska hurrying up the street, her brutish bodyguard thundering behind. I gulped. I wasn't sure how to explain the whole diamond mix-up debacle.

But Rulenska ran straight to Svetlanka and barrelled her into an embrace, tears streaming down both of their faces.

'Freeze!' the chief policeman called. He looked at his colleagues in confusion. Why were all these other people here? 'Didn't you all hear—?'

He didn't finish his sentence. For at that moment, two other voices butted in. Two familiar voices, saying something that I'd never in a million years expect them to say.

'I insist that you let my daughter and mother in,' Dad stated calmly. And there my parents were, beaming at all of us. 'I'm sure this whole' – he waved his hands at the armed police – '*thing* has been some sort of mix-up. Right?' A flicker of panic crossed his face as he took in the fact that his daughter and mother and some other people he'd never seen before in his life were surrounded by policemen.

I couldn't believe it. I peered closer – Mum and Dad looked years younger, and relaxed. Apart from the mild panic bit. 'Are you sure?' I whispered. 'You don't mind?'

Mum sniffed back tears. 'I'm sorry we didn't support you from the start,' she replied.

'I was worried about your granny's health,' Dad chipped in. 'I thought the strain of the journey would be too much, coupled with the rejection all over again. I couldn't bear to see it. That's why I was so against you coming here. But I believe in you both. Now I know you *have* to see this through.'

The security guard shared a grimace with the chief policeman. 'It's not that simple,' he frowned.

Before anyone could say anything, at that moment we heard the piercing sound of Tag's yaps coming from the front pocket of my dungarees. I felt him squirming around as he wriggled out from under my coat and scampered to the ground.

The chief policeman stepped backwards in surprise as Tag bounded over to him and started pawing at his legs. 'Get off!' the policeman cried, shaking his limbs vigorously.

'Tag!' I yelled. 'Stop it! You can't bite them!' *As much as I would love you to*, I thought to myself.

'Shoo! Shoo!!' the policeman cried. A few of his fellow officers raced to help him. Tag started leaping up at them too. The chief policeman batted Tag away with his hands and stumbled backwards . . .

. . . tripping right over the totally-pointless low iron gate at the edge of the pavement.

'Geearrrrggggh!' he cried as he tumbled backwards. He clutched at the other guards as he fell, dragging most of them down with him. They all landed flat on their backs on the cobbled street.

'Go, now,' Brian Ramsbottom hissed beside me as we all stared at the men on the ground. I couldn't help but think this all felt extraceedingly familiar.

Svetlanka, Chris P, Rulenska, her bodyguard, Mickey, Gertrude, the Hell's Angels and Mum and Dad nodded at me. They knew it was now or never.

Granny Joss and I turned towards the double doors and, with the surge of people behind us pushing us forward, we swarmed towards the security guard. He had no choice but to leap out of the way to avoid being crushed.

'Hey!' an uninjured policewoman shouted. 'Stop!'

But it was too late – Granny Joss and I were bustled through the doors of the City Hall.

Inside, the Nobel Prize chairman, a bespectacled gentleman whose tuxedo was clearly a size too small, for his buttons were strained and his cummerbund was about to ping off and go flying across the hall, stood on stage delivering his introduction. He was

only meant to give a quick 'welcome' before present-
ing the prizes to the six recipients. But so far, he'd
talked for twenty minutes about how *he* should have
been in the running for *all* of the awards. 'Nobel
Prize in Literature? I've been keeping a diary for
forty years. You should read that!' he boomed. The
audience may have hated it, but the fact that his
speech had gone on so long meant that no awards had
been given.

Until now.

The chairman cleared his throat and announced,
'Whatever. Moving on. The award for the Nobel
Prize in Literature goes to Sal—'

And it was at that precise moment that a terrific
commotion sounded from outside: the pounding of
footsteps of an army of people along the corridor.

A gruff voice crying, 'YOU CAN'T COME IN
HERE!' In three different languages, just to get the
message across.

The sound of a scuffle. The yap of a dog. The cries
of pain from several grown men.

And then—

The double doors burst open.

I took a moment to get my bearings, for it was dark inside the hall, and the lights from the stage were bright. Once my eyes had adjusted, I pegged it down the stairs to the front of the auditorium.

The audience gaped in astonishment as I was followed by an elderly lady with bright white hair, several Hell's Angels, a middle-aged couple holding hands, a glamorous diamond-clad flame-haired lady, a captain in a jaunty hat, his blonde-haired companion, a scruffy-looking dog and several police officers, some of whom were limping and clutching their backs.

I pointed up to the stage. 'IMPOSTOR!' I yelled as loud as I could. 'THAT MAN IS AN IMPOSTOR!'

I'd had the last thirty-one hours to practise what I was going to say. And, my gosh, it wasn't half dramatic.

The audience all gasped in shock at my outburst. The man on stage collecting his award stared, open-mouthed. 'I'm – I'm not an impostor,' he stuttered. 'I write all my own books!'

'Sorry,' I said apologetically, 'not you.' I pointed to Professor Smocks, seated in the middle of the stage. 'HIM!'

33

THE TRUTH WILL OUT

The audience all gasped in shock again.

Professor Smocks's face turned as purple as his suit. 'Wh-what do you mean?' he spluttered. 'I won the award fair and square.'

'Except you haven't, have you?' I cried. I motioned to Granny Joss standing behind me. 'Recognize this lady?'

Professor Smocks gulped. A flicker of panic crossed his face.

'Professor Joss – Jocelyn – Moore,' I stated as calmly as I could. Given that my knees were knocking together with nerves, this was no mean feat. 'She worked with you back at the Observatory in Greenwich, fifty years ago. And she discovered something, didn't she?'

Professor Smocks shrugged his shoulders. 'I don't know what you're talking about,' he blustered.

By this time, the chief policeman had recovered from his fall and called for attention once more. 'Stop!' he cried, glaring round at everyone. 'These people are wanted by the police!'

Everyone peered at me curiously. 'I can explain—' I started. I looked into the sea of people in the audience, and spotted in the front row a stern-looking bearded man wearing a crown. He must be the King of Sweden. 'I'll tell you everything about landing the hot-air balloon on top of the Eiffel Tower' – the audience gasped at that – '*afterwards*. But this is more important. Please.'

The King of Sweden looked from me to Granny Joss to the army of people behind me. He gave a curt nod of his head and whispered something to the man sitting next to him. The man sitting next to him whispered something to the woman next to *him*, who whispered something to the chief policeman.

The policeman let out a sigh, but then signalled to his officers to stand down. He waved his hand at me. 'Continue,' he commanded.

'My *granny* discovered that planet,' I declared, turning back to Professor Smocks on stage. 'Not you.

267

You lied to the world that *you* had found it, and that's why you're being given the award. Because you stole my granny's research and claimed it as your own. And quite frankly, it's not fair.'

Professor Smocks licked his lips, his eyes darting around the room as every single person in it stared up at him. 'Who do you think you are?' he demanded. 'Bursting in here, interrupting this lovely ceremony and throwing these wild accusations around? Do you really think *I* would steal? I've never even met the woman!'

I let out a puff of air. 'It's Thomas Thomas all over again,' I huffed. 'Except a million times worse. If his science trick was the best, then fine. The best should win. Not just someone who's a boy. And not just *not* me, because I'm a girl.'

I could tell I'd lost people there. But I *had* to make everyone see the truth. I delved into my rucksack and carefully picked out the hastily-put-together photographic glass plate.

'XT28E,' I declared, holding it up to the audience. 'You may know it as Planet Smocks *now*, but it was Granny Joss who first discovered it. Here's the picture she took of it. Look, see. It says "J. M." along the bottom.'

Professor Smocks's smile faded. 'Uh,' he stuttered, caught off-guard. 'Oh, um, let me see, oh, right, *that* Professor Moore. Oh, you should have said! Maybe, yes, I think I did work with her. It was years ago. I worked with a lot of people. You'll have to forgive my memory.' He ran a hand through his hair, trying to play it casual.

A small murmur spread through the audience as they took in Professor Smocks's backtrack. 'But that's all,' Professor Smocks called, keen to dampen the spark of doubt. 'I did NOT cheat or steal. I would never do that. Your granny could have taken that photo at any time. Yes, I'm sure she did. After I had shown everyone what I'd discovered. Half the people in the Observatory have one of those photos. I even have my own. Look. Trevor? Trevor! Where's my glass plate?'

Professor Smocks's put-upon PA, Trevor Foot, hurried up to the stage. His shabby green suit was crumpled, for he'd not had time to iron it, what with having to sort out all his boss's demands. He took a rectangular glass plate from his battered leather briefcase and held it out to Professor Smocks.

'Well then, little girl,' Professor Smocks declared, turning to me with a look of triumph on his face. 'Here's *my* glass plate. See? But if you're so sure she beat me to it, if you're so sure that your granny discovered the planet first, then where's your proof of *that*, hmm?' He knew he had me there.

Granny Joss stepped forward. It was the first time she'd spoken since we'd burst through the doors. She stood in front of Professor Smocks and looked him directly in the eyes. 'Tell me, Tarquin,' Granny Joss said, addressing Professor Smocks by his first name. He gulped at that. No one *ever* called him Tarquin. 'What date did you discover XT28E?' she asked, nodding to the glass plate he now held in his hands. 'And I'm talking the *exact* date. The one that's time-stamped along the bottom?'

Professor Smocks rolled his eyes. 'I don't have to prove myself to you.'

Granny Joss folded her arms and stared hard at him. '*I* discovered the planet. It took me months to carefully plot the course that a probe would one day take, let alone to work out the equation of how to get it there. The only reason you're here is because you claimed all of my work as your own. So yes, prove yourself to me if you think you know better.'

Professor Smocks glared at Granny Joss. He didn't know how to respond to her outburst.

He didn't have to. The chairman of the Nobel Prize committee coughed. 'Why don't you say it for our benefit, anyway?' he suggested, gesturing to the audience. 'Then we can get on with the dishing-out-awards business.'

Small beads of sweat gathered on Professor Smocks's forehead. 'Right,' he said. 'Um, well, it's quite small writing, actually—' he stuttered.

Everyone looked on in confusion. Why couldn't Professor Smocks tell them the exact date?

The Nobel Prize chairman strode across the stage and peered at Professor Smocks's glass plate. 'It says – the twenty-ninth of May, 1967,' he confirmed, squinting at the date stamp in the corner next to the initials 'T. N. I. S.'

'As I thought,' Granny Joss smiled. 'Matilda, could you be a dear and read out the date on *my* glass plate?'

My heart raced with excitement as I scoured the pieces of glass, looking for the one with the date on it. 'Got it!' I yelled after a moment. 'It says, the twenty-eighth of May, 1967.' The realization hit me like a ton of bricks. 'The twenty-*eighth* of May! The day before!'

'That's right,' Granny Joss nodded. 'Because, to my recollection,' she continued, turning once more to Professor Smocks, 'you were out of the office when I discovered the planet. It was late at night and I had to wait until you came into work the next morning to show you.'

'I don't think so,' Professor Smocks stuttered, ruffled. He cleared his throat. 'You're confusing things, that's all.'

A sudden thought occurred to Trevor Foot. 'Hang on a mo,' he called, delving into his briefcase once more. 'I can check!'

'WHAT?' Professor Smocks shrieked. He tugged at his swirly yellow cravat. He was getting rather hot under the collar.

Trevor Foot retrieved a huge battered book from within his briefcase. It *had* been a normal diary at one time, but it had had so many pages and keepsakes added to it over the years that it was now thicker than an A4 binder. 'Let me see,' Trevor murmured, 'the twenty-eighth of May, nineteen sixty— Ah, got it!' He rifled through a few pages. 'You were in meetings in Cleethorpes all day.'

'Nonsense!' Professor Smocks blustered. 'That can't be right. Look again.'

A shiver ran down Trevor Foot's spine as he re-read the page. After all the years Professor Smocks had belittled him. After *all* the times he'd had to clip his toenails – *he*, Trevor Foot, would be the one to bring about Smocks's downfall. 'Nope, it's all here,' he confirmed, trying to suppress a smile. 'I remember it well. You were trying to get funding for some project or other from the board members in Cleethorpes, and then we all went out for fish and chips on the beach afterwards. A crab bit you on the foot. You weren't back at the Observatory until the twenty-ninth.'

The Nobel Prize chairman peered at Professor Smocks curiously. I tried not to break out into a jig. Professor Smocks tried not to crumble. 'Um, it's – gosh it's warm in here,' he stuttered, forcing a laugh, but by now, the audience could see the look of alarm on his face. 'I – uh, could somebody please fetch me a glass of water?' Everyone was now looking at Professor Smocks. To his credit, he tried to maintain his outraged look. 'How – how dare you accuse me?' he blustered.

'It's all here in black and white!' I yelled.

'I simply won't have it,' Professor Smocks protested. He waggled his finger at the Nobel Prize chairman. 'This is no way to treat honoured guests. I shall be making a formal complaint!'

The Nobel Prize chairman looked from me to the photo, to Granny Joss, to Professor Smocks and back again. 'The evidence is pretty irrefutable,' he grimaced.

'*I* was in charge at the time,' Professor Smocks huffed. '*I* was the senior scientist. The Nobel Prize is mine!'

'Yes, but did you discover the planet in the first place?' the Nobel Prize chairman pressed. 'And do all the work?'

The blood drained from Professor Smocks's face. 'I-I . . .' he spluttered, lost for words. He looked out into the audience to see a thousand people staring back at him. This was it, then. The moment of truth. His shoulders sagged under the glare of the spotlight. 'Well, all right, no, I didn't do *that*—'

The audience gasped as one. Granny Joss let out a huge puff of air, years' worth of tension and pent-up anger releasing itself.

Tears welled in Professor Smocks's eyes. I couldn't help but feel a teensy bit sorry for him. What sort of man must he be to lie and cheat and claim credit for another person's work? Professor Smocks suddenly looked all of his eighty years, his eyes sunken and hollow.

And at that moment, I decided I was going to be kind. All right, he'd caused Granny Joss years of heartache over denying her contribution to science, and he'd lied through his teeth for the past half a century, but it was all out in the open now; I wasn't going to gloat and add to his misery.

I placed a comforting hand on his arm. 'I think I know what happened,' I said softly. 'I didn't win a science prize at school because people didn't think a girl could have invented The Handy-Handy-Hand, because I had to do some soldering and welding to make it. Did you say you discovered the planet because you knew no one would think Granny Joss could have?'

Professor Smocks looked at me thoughtfully. 'I guess you could say that,' he replied with sadness. 'I only ever wanted to make a difference. To *contribute*. There weren't many female scientists back then. And nobody took them seriously anyway. I knew no one would question me if I said *I'd* discovered the planet. I knew that everyone would question Jocelyn if she said she had.' He shrugged. 'That's just how it was in those days. I know that doesn't make it right.'

At that moment, something *wonderfully* unexpected happened. 'Absolutely it doesn't make it right!' a voice piped up from the audience. 'It's called The Matilda Effect.'

I peered into the darkness of the auditorium. 'Dad?'

He jogged up the stairs of the stage to join me. 'It's not right that my mum was denied her glory,' Dad said, addressing me, Professor Smocks and the packed

City Hall. 'Just because she's a woman and people believed Smocks over her. There's a name for it.' He reached into the back pocket of his suit trousers and produced a scrap of paper. '*The Matilda Effect*,' he read, '*is to deny the contribution of female scientists in research, instead attributing it to male colleagues*. It's happened more times than we'll ever know, not just with Mum. Saying, "That's just how it was in those days" isn't an excuse. Not for back then and not for now.' Dad placed a hand on my shoulder. 'Because it *still* happens,' he continued. 'My daughter's invention was the best at her school's science competition, but she wasn't awarded the prize because she's a girl and no one believed she could have made it on her own.' He turned to face me with tears in his eyes. 'Your mum and I have had time to think, love. We're sorry that we've never really understood what you do. But that doesn't mean you shouldn't do it. You've proved this past day that you can do anything! If anyone's got the perseverance and the guts and the sheer imagination to be an inventor, it's you. Never give up, Matilda!'

A lump formed in my throat. That was the nicest thing he'd ever said to me. Mum smiled up at us from the front row of the auditorium. 'We're so proud of you, darling,' she called. 'You didn't take no for an answer and you went out and *did* something!'

I embraced Dad in a hug. 'You're not going to kill me, then?'

'Oh, most definitely,' Dad said, trying to keep a straight face. 'You're grounded for running away and ignoring our attempts to contact you.' He squeezed my shoulder. 'But between you and me, we're mightily impressed.'

'Very good, very good,' the Nobel Prize chairman bustled, patting me and Dad on the back. 'But we've only rented the hall for a limited time, so . . .' Professor Smocks slumped back down in his seat as the chairman addressed the audience. 'I suppose we'd better give the award to its rightful owner,' he boomed. 'Ladies and gentlemen, I present the Nobel Prize in Physics, for the discovery of Planet Smocks—' he faltered. 'We'd better not call it that . . . Well, for discovering that planet anyway, and for charting the course of a probe to retrieve data from the furthest star known to man—'

'And women!' Dad interjected.

'Yes, yes,' the chairman ploughed on. 'Ladies and gentlemen, Professor Jocelyn Moore!'

The audience all got to their feet. Thunderous applause broke out as Granny Joss walked up the steps to the stage, a huge beam on her face. Tag barked enthusiastically and ran round in circles at all the commotion.

'Go, Granny!' I yelled as she made her way forward.

'Go, Mum!' Dad cried, punching the air.

'I'm *definitely* buying the film rights!' Brian Colin Ramsbottom called from the back of the auditorium.

My heart swelled as the chairman presented Granny Joss with her trophy and she took a bow to rapturous applause. This, without a shadow of a doubt, was the very best moment of my life. I was so pleased my parents were there to share it too.

As Dad and I headed down the steps of the stage, Granny Joss did something remarkable. She moved to Professor Smocks, who was sitting in quiet despair, his head in his hands. 'I forgive you, Tarquin,' she said simply, patting his arm.

And like that, fifty years of heartache melted away.

The audience quietened down. There were still a few more awards to be given yet. I felt sorry for the remaining recipients – there was no way another winner would get the same reaction that Granny Joss did.

As we walked down the aisle of the auditorium, a tall thin lady stood up from her seat and held out her hand. 'Hello,' she said.

Mum and Dad let out a gasp of surprise. 'Prime Minister!' Dad said.

'It's an honour to meet you,' she said to Granny Joss. She peered down at me with interest. 'So, you're the little girl who sent me the email?'

Dad's jaw practically hit the floor. I shook the Prime Minister's hand heartily. 'That's me,' I said. A thought whizz-popped into my brain. Even though we'd achieved so much, I couldn't resist doing one final thing. I reached into my rucksack and pulled out The Handy-Handy-Hand. 'This is my finest invention,' I explained. 'I mentioned it in my email.' The Prime Minister nodded enthusiastically as I ran through the various functions of the device.

From the corner of my eye, I spotted Dad looking at The Handy-Handy-Hand curiously, as if he was only really seeing it for the first time.

'What an excellent piece of engineering,' the Prime Minister marvelled. 'We could do with some of these in the office. Why don't you all come to afternoon tea and show this to my team? We may well commission you to make some more. Would that be all right?'

I nodded. If by 'the office' she meant '10 Downing Street', that would be fine by me. And a commission? That'd show Thomas Thomas! At this rate, I wouldn't have to eat vegetarian pasta bake for eight years to save for an international patent! Yazooks!

The Prime Minister patted me on the back. 'It's girls like you who are the future of our country,' she said. 'We need more Matildas inventing things, let me tell you.'

Granny Joss leaned in to hug me. 'Mission accomplished, dearie,' she whispered. 'For justice!'

'For justice!' I murmured.

'Uh, excuse me!' a voice commanded at the back of the auditorium. The chief policeman glowered at me.

I'd forgotten he was there. 'You're still in trouble for landing a hot-air balloon on top of the Eiffel Tower.'

I opened my mouth to try to explain, but the Prime Minister waved her hand at him. 'Leave that with me,' she called across the hall. 'I'll speak to your boss about it. You're dismissed.'

The chief policeman couldn't believe what he was hearing. The King of Sweden whispered to the man next to him, who whispered to the woman next to *him*, who stood up from her seat and shouted, '*Du kan gå.*' I've no idea what she said, but after a moment, the chief of police let out a deep sigh and trudged out of the hall.

Yessssss!!! It looked like we weren't going to be in terrible trouble for the whole hot-air balloon debacle after all. Thanks, Prime Minister! Maybe I really *will* vote for you one day!

At that moment, a teary-eyed Rulenska ran up to us and barrelled me into a hug. 'You did it!' she cried.

I gulped. She seemed happy, but there was still the small matter of her stolen diamonds. 'Um, we didn't mean to smuggle your diamonds out of the circus,' I said. 'It was the clown and the contortionist.'

Mum and Dad stared on, open-mouthed.

Rulenska nodded simply. 'I know everything,' she soothed. 'I've got someone tracking them down as we speak. But I've decided,' she confessed, leaning in closer to Granny Joss and me, 'that I don't want to be involved in criminal proceedings any more. I'm going to open my own bakery, making Grandmama's easy-peasy-lemon-and-orange-marmalade-and-leftover-bits-of-old-tea-bag fruit cake. You've inspired me. You've inspired *us*.' She gestured to Svetlanka a few rows back. 'We're going into business together.'

As everyone started walking away, out of the hall and out of our lives, I wondered how my family and I were going to get home. We hadn't really thought about that bit.

The Prime Minister patted me on the shoulder again. 'I say,' she smiled. 'Rather than driving home, would you like to join me and fly back in my private jet?'

I didn't need asking twice. 'Yes, please,' I said. 'It'll be the best form of transport we've taken yet!'

Everyone laughed at that. 'Better than a comedy dog mini-van too,' Dad agreed.

'Oh, and one final thing,' the Prime Minister said. 'We'll need to change the name of the planet. Can't have it as Planet Smocks now, obviously. How about Planet Jocelyn?'

I tingled with pride. How amazing would that be?

'No,' Granny Joss said firmly, shaking her head.

'No?' the Prime Minister asked, confused.

'No?' I repeated.

'NO?' Dad boomed.

'I'd rather call it something else,' Granny Joss explained. 'Something more fitting. How about' – she looked down at me in delight – 'Planet Matilda.'

My heart swelled with love and gratitude at that. Have I mentioned before that my granny's amazing?

'All right,' the Prime Minister said, nodding enthusiastically. 'Planet Matilda it is.'

Ha! Take *that*, Thomas Thomas! Take *that*, Mr Yonker and Mr Varney and Mr Dorfman and your one thousand pounds' worth of dog food vouchers!

Remember how I couldn't find a quote about brilliant female scientists? Here, have this:

If I can get Granny Joss to Sweden without a plan – or a passport, may I add – then I can do anything I put my mind to.

Said by me. All right I'm not a brilliant scientist but really, there's no stopping me. The Prime Minister might commission me to make more Handy-Handy-Hands. I'm going to be a famous inventor! It's onwards and upwards for Matilda Moore!

Tears welled up in my eyes as I thought about everything that had happened in the last thirty-one hours. Who would have thought our travels would take us on a boat to Calais, in a taxi to Criel-sur-Mer, in a hot-air balloon with a fake-French celebrity to Paris, in a sleek silver car to Hamburg, to the circus with a poisoned lion, on a train to Denmark with a contortionist in a suitcase, or in a convoy of Hell's Angels on motorbikes to Sweden? We'd reunited a gangster with her long-lost sister. We'd encouraged a film star to be true to himself. We were flying home in a private jet. Granny Joss had her Nobel Prize. I had a dog.

'It must be the end,' I whispered to myself, looking around at everybody, taking in their happy, joyous faces. 'Because everything, but everything, has worked out all right.'

And, goodness knows, it doesn't get any better than that.

MATILDA MOORE'S
INVENTORS
INVENTORY

Remember I said I was going to make a list of all the brilliant inventors and scientists and engineers and people in history who had changed the world? Well, without further ado, you lucky lot, here are my favourites:

Rachel Zimmerman

In 1984, Rachel created a software program called Blissymbols that allowed non-speaking people, like those with disabilities, to communicate. People would point to symbols on a board using a special touch pad and then the Blissymbol programme translated them into writing, so everyone could read what they were trying to say on the screen. Oh, by the way, she was twelve when she invented this, for a science project at school, but it was so good she ended up with the silver medal at the World Exhibition of Young Inventors. The winner that year must have been for inventing fire or something, because how did it beat Rachel's Blissymbols??

Tim Berners-Lee

He's not a woman, but he created the internet, so we'll let him off. His full name is: Sir Timothy John Berners-Lee OM KBE FRS FREng FRSA FBCS. Take that, Professor Smocks!

Sarah E. Goode

When we flew home on the Prime Minister's private jet, I pressed a little button which signalled to the flight attendant that I'd like another bag of peanuts. (I did this three times. Mum told me off for being greedy.) But I discovered that the lady who invented the 'Signal Chair' device that went on to be used like this on aeroplanes was Miriam Benjamin, who was the *second* African-American woman ever to be granted a US patent for her invention. The *first* was Sarah E. Goode, who invented a folding cabinet bed in 1885. *Necessity is the mother of invention!* Sarah wanted to help people who lived in tiny homes and flats (Dad says, 'Well that's most people in New York City, then') and she designed a bed that could be folded away and used as a desk and for storage when it wasn't being slept in. I think she should be called Sarah E. VERY Goode. Ha ha ha.

Stephanie Kwolek

An American chemist, best known for inventing a synthetic fibre that's extraceedingly strong called poly-paraphenylene terephtalamide. It's also known as Kevlar, which is used in bulletproof vests and car tyres. She was only the fourth woman to be added to the National Inventors Hall of Fame. (I'm going to be in that one day, you know.)

Jocelyn Bell Burnell

Is an astrophysicist who, in 1967, discovered the very first radio pulsar (a neutron star that emits a beam of electromagnetic radiation). But it was her boss at the time who won the Nobel Prize in Physics for the discovery, even though *he* hadn't discovered it. DOES ANY OF THIS SOUND FAMILIAR?

Rosalind Franklin

When she was fifteen, Rosalind decided to become a scientist, even though her parents didn't want her to. She learned how to take X-ray images of DNA fibres, which is the information in our bodies that we use to build cells. Her photos led to James Watson and Francis Crick discovering the actual structure of DNA, and guess who won the Nobel Prize in Physiology for that? (Clue: it wasn't Rosalind Franklin.)

There's a pattern emerging here, isn't there?

Tu Youyou

Science saves lives, people! In the 1970s, Dr Youyou discovered a drug called *artemisinin* which she used to treat malaria, a tropical disease spread by pesky mosquitoes. Artemisinin was regarded as one of the best breakthroughs in tropical medicine of the twentieth century and has been used to save the lives of *millions* of people around the world. Tu Youyou became the first Chinese person to win the Nobel Prize in Physiology or Medicine, which was probably the icing on the cake for her. What with, you know, SAVING MILLIONS OF LIVES AND EVERYTHING!

Deepika Kurup

Another woman saving lives is Deepika, who invented a solar-powered water purification system. It provides fresh, clean water worldwide, which is particularly brilliant for places that don't have it. Also, clean water helps to stop diseases spreading, so I bet Tu Youyou is well pleased. AND Deepika's only nineteen, which is only a *little* bit older than me. AND she won lots of awards for her invention, including the 2014 US Stockholm Junior Water Prize. I bet she didn't have to fly a hot-air balloon to get there, though.

Helen Sharman

Everyone raves about Tim Peake being the first British astronaut to fly to the International Space Station, but in 1991, Helen Sharman became the first *ever* British astronaut to fly into space, and the first woman to visit the Mir space station. She also once worked as a chemist for Mars Incorporated, which means she's been into space *and* got paid to eat chocolate. What a gal!

I'd better include some more men too, so you don't think I'm being mean.

Alfred Nobel

He was a Swedish chemist and engineer who invented dynamite. His family owned a business producing weapons for the Crimean War in the 1850s, but one day a shed used for the preparation of nitroglycerine (a heavy, colourless, explosive liquid that's a major component of gunpowder) blew up, killing five people, including Alfred's younger brother. So Alfred invented dynamite, which was a safer substance to handle than nitroglycerine. (I still wouldn't recommend touching it, though.) After a lifetime of blowing things up and causing so much destruction, he wanted to be remembered for better things, so created the Nobel Prizes to honour progress across different scientific fields.

Leonardo da Vinci

The famous fifteenth-century painter who invented things so far ahead of his time. He spent his days sketching out diagrams for what we now know as the parachute, helicopter, machine gun, diving suit, armoured tank, ball bearings and the world's first robotic knight. Yazooks! In his spare time, he painted the *Mona Lisa,* the world's most famous painting. He died aged sixty-seven, probably in need of a rest.

Insert Your Name Here

Why not try inventing something? Don't worry what other people think of you – I don't care that I get funny looks when eating my vegetarian pasta bake at school every day. Just try it! (Inventing, not my vegetarian pasta bake. I wouldn't wish that on anyone.) There are no limits to your imagination! And don't be afraid to fail! Every time something goes wrong, it's a chance to learn what to do right the next time. Fail again, but fail better. Remember Thomas Edison and his 1000-step light bulb, people!

Oh, one final thing. Thanks so much for reading my book. Incidentally, the world's first-ever novel was called *The Tale of Genji*, written in the early eleventh century by . . . yep, a woman. Naturally.

I'll stop banging on about it now. You get the point.

AMAZING SCIENCE TRICKS TO DAZZLE YOUR FRIENDS!

The entrants of Arnos Yarm Comprehensive's Science Competition had good ideas for their science tricks; they just didn't know what they were doing.

Have no fear, my friends, of being laughed at up on stage like Thomas Thomas if you follow my simple instructions. (You might want to put on some goggles. And maybe some gloves. And maybe put newspaper down on the floor so your mum doesn't shout, 'MATILDA! [*insert your name here*] THAT'S THE SECOND TIME THIS WEEK YOU'VE BURNED THE CARPET!')

Ready?

HOW TO MAKE A PAPIER-MÂCHÉ VOLCANO

You will need:

- A large cardboard box
- Scissors
- A small empty plastic drinks bottle (without lid)
- Glue
- A bowl
- Water
- Newspaper
- Paints and paintbrushes
- A funnel or rolled-up paper
- Bicarbonate of soda (also known as baking soda)
- Some red food colouring
- Vinegar

1. Cut a large square out of your cardboard box to make the base board.

2. Stick the bottom of the drinks bottle to the base board with glue.

3. In a bowl, create a mixture of thin white glue and water.

4. Scrunch up some of the sheets of newspaper, dunk them fully in the glue mixture and stick them onto the cardboard round the base of the bottle. Keep building up the volcano.

5. Rip half of the newspaper into 2 centimetre-wide strips and add these in layers onto the drinks bottle on top of the scrunched-up newspaper. Your volcano should be taking shape by now.

6. Once the newspaper is completely dry, use paint to decorate the volcano.

Now for the really fun bit (but BEWARE – it gets a bit messy):

1. Using the funnel, pour 3 tablespoons of bicarbonate of soda into the drinks bottle.

2. If you've got it, you can add red food colouring here to colour the lava.

3. Finally – get ready for your volcano to erupt – add the vinegar (up to a cup's worth if you *really* want to see it explode) and STAND BACK!

Adding vinegar to bicarbonate of soda causes a chemical reaction, creating carbonic acid which is an *unstable substance*. That's why there's so much fizz. TA-DA!

MAKING AN EGG FLOAT IN WATER

An egg sinks to the bottom if you drop it into an ordinary glass of water. But here's how to make an extraceedingly unordinary one!

You will need:

- Water
- A tall glass
- Salt
- One egg

1. Pour the water into the glass until it's about half full (Granny Joss calls me an optimist).
2. Stir in lots of salt – about 6 tablespoons (that's the big spoon) should do it, I reckon. Make sure it's all dissolved.

3. Gently lower the egg into the water.
4. Do not drop the egg over Mr Keegan's brown shoes.

The egg will float in the water because of density! Like when Granny Joss told me how hot-air balloons work. Because salt water is denser than drinking water, the egg doesn't sink to the bottom like it normally does. What an amazing trick! (As long as you put something *in* the water and don't hold up just the glass to your audience. YES, I'M TALKING ABOUT YOU, JOSH!)

THE EXPLODING
BAG TRICK!

OK, so *technically* this wasn't an entry in the Science Competition, but it would have been so handy throughout our journey, so I'll share it anyway. It's awesome and it involves gas (and not the smelly kind that comes after a curry).

You will need:

- 1/2 cup of vinegar (if there's any left over from the papier-mâché volcano)
- A sandwich bag – one of those ziplock ones would be ace
- A tissue (doesn't have to be one of your mum's lavender-scented ones)
- Bicarbonate of soda (our old friend again)

1. Pour the vinegar into the sandwich bag and zip it closed.
2. Lay the tissue flat and place 4 teaspoons (the little one, but a big heap per spoonful) of bicarbonate of soda into the centre of it.
3. Fold the corners of the tissue to enclose the bicarbonate of soda in a little bundle.
4. Unzip the sandwich bag to fit the tissue/soda bundle inside and quickly close the bag again.
5. Shake it up until it fizzes.
6. When it starts to fizz, put it down and wait for it to explode. You might want to stand back. And tighten your science goggles!

Just like with the volcano, the vinegar mixing with the bicarbonate of soda causes a chemical reaction and creates carbon dioxide. This needs room to expand and, as it does so, the bag is forced to explode.

I TOLD YOU IT WAS AWESOME!

ONE LAST THING
BEFORE YOU GO . . .

Are you still here? EXCELLENT! Thanks for reading *all* the way to the end. I don't sometimes, because I get distracted if I'm reading a book about a boy wizard or something and an idea pops into my head and I have to put the book down to sketch it out (*What if you modified a hairdryer on the end of the kitchen mop to make a real flying broomstick?*) and then I forget where I am in the story and I start a new one. So thanks for not doing that.

Granny Joss discovered Planet Matilda when she worked at the Royal Observatory in Greenwich. It houses the Great Equatorial Telescope, the largest telescope in the UK, and it helped scientists like my granny to make huge discoveries in the field of astrophysics. It's no longer a working laboratory, but you can still go and visit it as a museum. Granny Joss and I are going back there next month, so we can show off her Nobel Prize and get a plaque put up in her name. We're extraceedingly excited.

It's all made me want to know more about stars and planets too – and not just the ones in *our* solar system. I can name all those already, and some of their moons.

I can also point out The Plough in the night sky. It's a pattern (also known as an *asterism*) of the seven brightest stars in the Ursa Major constellation. It looks a bit like a shopping trolley, or, well, a plough, because it's four stars in a rectangle and three stars in the shape of the trolley handle. It's the easiest thing to spot in the sky, I reckon. I can also find Orion's Belt and the North Star. If *I* were you, I'd be trying to find them too next time you get a clear night because, you know what? It's properly brilliant and makes you realize there's a big wide universe out there and *endless* possibilities.

And all of this – the science tricks, the inventing, the engineering, The Handy-Handy-Hand, how hot-air balloons work, the exploding bag, astrophysics, curing a poisoned lion, making glue, the Clifton

Suspension Bridge, eroding money in a bottle of Coke, observing the stars – it *all* falls under the topic of science. So if you think you want to be a scientist, well, my friend, lucky you, because there's just SO MUCH you can do.

SO WHAT ARE YOU WAITING FOR?

Acknowledgements

Thank you to everyone at Penguin Random House – particularly Kirsten Armstrong for the initial idea and encouragement to run with it; and to Natalie Doherty, Sue Cook and Frances Evans for making it so much stronger. Thank you to Matt Jones for a tremendous front cover design!

Thank you to the wonderful team at United Agents for your patience, support and enthusiasm – a huge hoorah to Jodie Hodges, Jane Willis and Emily Talbot.

Thanks to Donna de Haan for informing me about Dutch delicacies!

To NANJAS and the Only Connect sub-team. What a bunch of legends you are!

To my LCC and writer's group – thanks for all your (at times brutally honest) feedback.

As I was writing this book, I was inspired by so many amazing, creative, funny and smart women in history and those that I'm lucky enough to call my friends. Hats off to Nikki, Michela, Helen, Katy and Molly, Candice and Amy, the SHSG gang and Bake Off crew.

To my family – Mum, Dad, Andrew, Charlotte (sorry there's a bit of lying in this one), Lily and last, but NOT least, Barney.

Finally, to my husband, Rik. Thanks for your unwavering support and cheerleading, you thoroughly good egg, you.

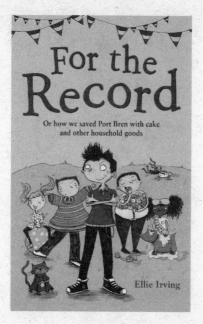

For the
Record

Or how we saved Port Bren with cake
and other household goods

Ellie Irving

Loudest burp?
Freckliest face?
Fastest time to superglue
hand to head?

Luke loves world records. He knows everything about
them – the hairiest man alive, the woman with the most
tattoos, even the world's most venomous snake.

When Luke finds out his tiny village is going to be
bulldozed to the ground, he concocts a brilliant plan to make
Port Bren famous – by getting the eccentric villagers to break
fifty world records. In a week.

The clock is ticking.
And the records just keep getting crazier . . .

For Queen. For Country. For Dad.

Dear Your Majesty,

My name is Billie Templar. I live in Merchant Stanton,
which is all right, but it's not as nice as Buckingham
Palace, I bet. Anyway, I know you're really busy, what
with being Queen, but I have a favour to ask you.

Please can you send my dad home from the war? He's
been out there for the last eleven weeks. His best
friend got blown up today, and I don't want him to get
hurt, so please can you excuse him from the fighting?

Billie

How do you make yourself heard in the midst of chaos?

Anthony Button loves his big family,
but their noise can drive him crazy.
And with the arrival of a brand-new older brother,
it's worse than ever!

So Ant starts a silent protest to try and get everyone's attention.
But now he's pressed the mute button, will he ever
find his voice again?

WARNING!

THIS STORY CONTAINS:

– A sheep called Alan Shearer. Even though she's a she
– The greatest illusion trick known to man!
– DASTARDLY crooks
– A pesky big brother
– A 1000-piece *Lord of the Rings* jigsaw puzzle with all the
pieces making up Gandalf's face missing
– Shear determination
– A brave young hero. Yep, that's me.
Charlie Rudge, aged 10 and ¾ . . .

READ ON IF EWE DARE!